Seekers Finders Finders Keepers

Find The Ancient Path

Jennifer Phillips

Title: Find The Ancient Path
Series: Seekers Finders Finders Keepers
Author & Illustrator: Jennifer Kathleen Phillips
Publisher: Wing To Wing
Mount Nathan, Queensland, Australia
Copyright 2018 Jennifer Kathleen Phillips
ISBN: 10:0975195875
ISBN: 13:978-0-9751958-7-1
National Library of Australia Cataloguing-in-Publication Dewey Number: A823.4
Ebook: ISBN-13: 978-0-9751958-8-8
Website: www.jenniferphillips.com.au

Other books by the author:
2012   I want to travel with you
2012   Word Power Poetry and Poetics
2011   Israel Photographed
2004   You Can Make A Website
2000   © 2000 From New Zealand
1995   In Their Likeness
1992   In His Hands
1983   In His Time

Some place names are real and some aren't.
Bible verses are the author's translations from Greek and Hebrew.

Acknowledgements

I want to thank my sister Susan Legg for allowing me to use photos of her as the model for my images of Haras. Thanks also to Joshua Thiele and Natalie Phillips for allowing me to use their images for Nen and Ahsha respectively.

A number of friends and family members, including my husband Peter, daughter Natalie, Kathryn Thiele, Marion Martineer and Iola Goulton read the draft, edited it, and made suggestions, which I appreciate greatly. Thirteen year-old Tara also read the first draft and made some helpful suggestions, as did Sinead.

I acknowledge Jesus who has inspired me, taught me and led me along the journey of making this novel. I've enjoyed the process, and pray that you will not only enjoy it, but be blessed by Jesus, as you read it.

Contents

Chapter A 1
Chapter B 10
Chapter C 20
Chapter D 27
Chapter E 32
Chapter F 42
Chapter G 53
Chapter H 65
Chapter I 75
Chapter J 87
Chapter K 94
Chapter L 100
Chapter M...107
Chapter 14 113
Chapter 15 119
Chapter 16 124
Chapter 17 129
Chapter 18 134
Chapter 19 142
Chapter 20 146
Chapter 21 154
Chapter 22 162
Chapter 23 171
Chapter 24 177
Chapter 25 183
Chapter 26 190
Chapter 27 197
Chapter N 202
Chapter O 209
Chapter P 215

Chapter Q 220
Chapter R...226
Chapter S 236
Chapter T 240
Chapter U 245
Chapter V 250
Chapter W 257
Chapter X...262
Chapter Y...268
Chapter Z...273
Questions 281
Meaning of Names 282
The Hiding Song...283
Author Bio 284

The literary device called alphabetical acrostics has been used in this novel, and a message hidden in the middle. You will need to check out the first letter of each chapter from 14-27, to find the message.

Chapter

Accusing voices stalked her in the darkness.

"No-one will find you here. No-one."

Haras swung her last match wildly. Who was following her? She wanted to run but her feet wouldn't move. The flame was burning her fingers, but she held on. Where was the door?

"Sarah, Sarah." The words were a breeze on her cheek. How she wished it was her name, but it wasn't. The match went out. She tried to scream but couldn't. No sounds would come from her mouth.

"What's my name? What's my name?"

Haras woke suddenly. She couldn't roll over. The sheets were twisted around her. She wiped the sweat from her neck and pulled at them.

Again! That awful dream. She didn't want to wake up to it, today of all days. Haras reached for the clock. Ten thirty. She flopped back remembering something someone had yelled into her ear the night before.

"Last year as a teen. What're you gonna do about it … more parties?"

Haras tried to remember his name. She couldn't. He was one of Ahsha's many friends. She sure had invited a lot, mostly from Hobart. Haras knew some of them from school, but she'd been too busy to socialize much and had lost touch. She had to work and study. Who else would pay her bills? Anyway, she loved her subject. Horticulture. Maybe she could become self-sufficient …

The music still blared in her head, and flashes of the dream disturbed her. Haras had to get up. She swung her legs over the side of the bed. Her fluffy slippers lay at her feet. She slid into them and padded to the bathroom.

Her tongue felt dry and furry. She poked it out expecting it to look like her slippers. She glared at her reflection in the mirror. Not even dark rings under her eyes. Her reflection was lying. It didn't look like she felt … well maybe her hair did. Thick dark clumps were waving in all directions. She combed them with her fingers.

Haras yawned her way into the kitchen and stopped by the china cabinet. She frowned at a chipped brown vase of drooping flowers. The Gerbera's had been crying out for attention for days. She *would* get around to it, but not now, and the vase? Maybe it was time to throw that out too, only it was her first attempt at pottery. Beside them was a photo of her and her mother at Franklin Wharf. It took her back there, listening to the seagulls, leaning in close for a selfie. The memory pushed the angst from her mind and she smiled. She had so few photos of them together. Her mother had always been too busy.

Haras felt a hand on her shoulder. She jumped. She hadn't even heard Ahsha come into the room. Ahsha was already dressed - designer jeans and pink blouse. Everything she wore looked a million dollars. No sign of the party hanging on.

"You're up," Haras said. "I thought you were still asleep."

"No, been outside soaking up the sun and the mountain view. So much nicer than looking at our neighbour's house. Anyway, didn't want to wake you." Ahsha peered at the photo.

Haras turned away and filled a glass with water. She took a long slow drink. "So that's why you look as fresh as the mountain breeze."

Ahsha gave a half laugh. "Do I?"

Haras rubbed her eyes and ran her fingers through her hair again.

"… and smell like roses. I haven't even brushed my hair," she said.

Ahsha tossed her head and grinned. "Didn't notice. Must be the breeze in my eyes."

Haras turned and leaned forward to stare into Ahsha's eyes. "Hmmm. No, all I see is an ocean."

They both laughed and Ahsha glanced back at the photo. "So what's it like to be nineteen?"

Haras elbowed her. "You'll know in a few months. Thanks for all the help with the party, and for staying over."

"No prob. I thought it might help, being the first anniversary. What did you think of Ara? He had eyes for you last night."

"Is that his name? Na. Not really my type, anyway I haven't got time."

"It's been a year, Haras. You could squeeze one in now and then. There's a cute new intern at work ..."

"Oh Ahsha, as if someone like that would go for someone who hasn't got her life together. If he asked me about my family I might burst into tears and embarrass him."

"You haven't for months." Ahsha touched the photo. "Haven't seen this photo before. When was it taken?"

"A week before Mum died. Mum was trying out her new mobile phone." Haras bit her bottom lip.

"You both look so different. I mean ..."

"Yeah. I know what you mean." Haras tapped her lips. "We have the same lips, same eye colour. That's all, I suppose."

"You have such beautiful blue eyes—stunning with your olive complexion. You should've taken your sunglasses off."

Haras appreciated her praise even though it was something she was often told, and it wasn't the first time Ahsha had mentioned her eyes. In comparison, Ahsha looked like a model, a blonde blue-eyed beauty. Haras couldn't compare.

"I suppose I take after my father's side of the family." Haras sighed.

"The Mediterranean look?"

"Yep. I don't have Mum's fair skin, that's for sure." Haras tilted her head.

"Shame you never met your Dad. Did you find a photo of him? I mean in your mother's things."

Haras waved her hands. She wanted to push the task away. "Still haven't had the energy to go through all her stuff."

"Want me to help?"

It wasn't the first time Ahsha had offered, but Haras wasn't ready, even though it was a whole year since her mother's death. The very thought of all her mother's stuff made Haras feel like her name—harassed about many things. Now some of those harassing thoughts popped into her mind again. She was alone. No relatives as far as she knew, not even a cousin. Her stomach tightened.

Ahsha glanced in Haras's direction, but Haras kept her eyes glued to the photo.

"Your mother had such a cute little nose."

"Yeah. Suppose that's what really set us apart … my long nose and her snub one." Haras forced a grin. "Mum said too many people pressed her nose when she was little, saying, 'What a lovely little button nose you have, so it stayed like that!'" Haras loved her mother's explanation.

Ahsha giggled. "That's so funny." She leaned in for a closer look.

Haras turned away. She wanted to end the photo conversation, but didn't. "It makes Mum look kinda rounded, though." She never thought of her mother as a rounded kind of person. Sometimes she even admired her sharp tongue and wit.

Haras could almost feel the stiff white hospital sheets as she pictured her mother lying there—dying there. She'd moved in close to hear her last raspy words.

"Finders keepers. Gran was right. I shouldn't have hidden it."

For a moment, her mother's pale face had relaxed into the white of the pillow. Suddenly her eyes had opened again.

"Please. Tell Deerg … I'm sorry."

She was barely coherent.

"The pot … you must find him … tell him … I'm sorry … his heirloom … Jesus …"

Haras held her breath. Jesus?

Her mother's eyes had fluttered open again. "Sorry." She took a few laboured breaths and suddenly there'd been nurses everywhere.

Ahsha poked her. "You still there?"

Haras poked her back. "Just!"

"See all this family talk and no tears. You've got it together, girl. I could arrange a double date. You me …"

"Don't you dare. I've got a pile of uni assignments to work on." Haras scratched her head.

Ahsha turned and pointed towards a shelf of recipe books. "Is that little urn new?"

"Urn?" Haras's gaze followed Ahsha's manicured finger to a small pot, tarnished like an old penny. "Oh the pot. No, can't you see it's ancient?"

Haras couldn't help the tease as she bumped against Ahsha. "See those etchings? Hieroglyphics. How old do you think they are?"

Ahsha bumped her back. "I meant …"

"I found it a few weeks ago. Mum said my father, Deerg gave it to her. Apparently, he didn't believe in rings or marriage. He told her rings were a symbol of slavery and a partner should be a queen, not a slave."

"Well, that's a novel idea."

"Yes, but a pot?" Haras starred past Ahsha. "He was offering Mum a place in his family story … by sharing his treasure, Mum said."

Ahsha pulled out a bar stool from the island bench and ran her hand along the white leather before sitting. "That's so sweet."

Haras took the pot down and handed it to Ahsha. "Yeah. I like the idea too."

Ahsha turned the pot around in her hand, before placing it on the bench. "It's a strange heirloom. Maybe someone's ashes were important." She opened the lid.

Haras shook her head. "There aren't any. Mum never mentioned any. She called it a pot."

Ahsha twisted the lid firmly back in place. "Feel like coffee? I'll make it if you like." She pointed to the drooping flowers. "You can deal with those."

"Mmm. Thanks. A bit off, aren't they?" Haras said.

Ahsha began filling the coffee machine with fresh water. She nodded. "More than a bit."

Haras took a plastic bag from the pantry and lifted one of the dead Gerbera's from the vase. Her mouth puckered as she pulled away from the foul smell. Holding her breath, she placed them, one by one in the bag. Task completed, she breathed easily and carried them outside.

"Promises, promises," she said, as she threw them into the compost bin. Her parents had thrown their forever promises away, just like dead flowers.

According to her mother, her father was always looking for easy ways to get rich quick. Someone had duped him into chasing gold, the opportunity of a lifetime. He was a seeker on the 'S-e-h-c-i-r journey.' Haras had always ended her mother's story by saying, "You don't have to remind me. It's riches spelt back to front … and … he missed one opportunity."

Haras couldn't help pulling her head back as she remembered how often she'd tried to avoid her mother patting her head as she said, "I have some of his hidden treasure right here!"

For the umpteenth time, Haras wished her mother hadn't hidden her from her father. She lifted the rubbish bin lid, dropped the bag in. But where was her father now? How could she tell him her mother was sorry and wanted him to know he had a daughter? Haras wanted him to know too, but she wanted more than that, she wanted to know him.

Chapter 11

Blinking at the brightness of the sunlight outside reminded Haras of the time. It was nearly lunchtime and she was still in her blue-to-match-her-eyes pyjamas. She yawned. Oh well, what did it matter? She didn't have to be anywhere.

"Coffee's ready!" Ahsha yelled from inside.

Haras ambled back towards the house, almost stubbing her toes against the concrete doorstep. She closed the door and leaned into it as she looked at her new bracelet. She ran her finger over the silver word: Love. Ahsha had given it to her.

"Do you like it?"

Haras jumped. "Yes, it's the best Ahsha. Thanks." She more than liked it. She loved it. "A perfect birthday present."

"I'm glad. I hoped it would cheer you up. We do love you, y'know."

"I know." Her Gran's words popped into her mind.

Chasing after riches is an ancient dreaming. It's a journey fraught with dangers and regrets.

"Ok, I saw that." Ahsha said as she gave Haras a mug of coffee.

"Is that actually a smile? Spill the beans."

Haras drank in the smell of her coffee. "Mmm." She took a sip. "Something my gran used to say." She almost laughed. Gran had warned her more than once about chasing after things that belong in this world. She repeated Gran's words to Ahsha.

"Your gran was right. Life's too short to chase after things that aren't eternal. Come on. My coffee's getting cold in the kitchen."

"Well Gran ..." Haras looked at the ceiling as she followed Ahsha down the hall. She held out her bracelet. "I wouldn't regret chasing after a few more of these treasures."

"You don't need to chase after that. Put it on your Christmas list! Maybe my Santa-Dad can find another one for your stocking this year—a necklace to match maybe?"

Ahsha's Dad was the best. She had enjoyed camping trips with him and Ahsha.

"You're never too old to camp," he always said. The first time he said it, Haras couldn't imagine her grandmother camping, or even her mother and she'd told him so.

Haras grinned again. It was strange what she remembered. Her gran had often told her she was a real treasure. Her mother had as well. If her real father had known about her, she felt sure he would've come back to treasure her too. He might even have regretted their break up as her mother had. Oh well … She leaned towards a square glass vase of yellow roses on the kitchen island, and inhaled their fragrance.

"Mmm. Say thanks to your dad from me … for the roses. And the vase is just perfect. I love chunky glass." Haras winced at Ahsha's frown.

"You can tell him yourself. Phone him."

Haras nodded. "Yes, I should." She cupped her coffee and took a sip.

Ahsha pulled the fridge door open. "You should." She shook her head. Nothing in the fridge. Anything yummy hidden away somewhere?"

"I wish!" Haras opened the pantry door. "Only healthy stuff here. Sorry. Oh, I forgot. Chocolates! They're in the lounge."

Haras found the half-eaten box of soft centred chocolates, and offered them to Ahsha, before relaxing back into the white leather couch. It needed a clean. Her mother had always kept it spotless. Well, as spotless as one could with a teenage daughter and her friends. She wasn't as diligent, even though she wanted to be. Haras squirmed as a memory flashed into her head. She shook it away and concentrated on Ahsha. "Sorry. I'm not much company today am I?"

Ahsha put her mug down and flicked at a speck on her jeans. "That's why I'm here." She began inspecting her newly manicured nails.

Haras looked at her own fingernails. She'd given them a good scrub before her party, but they still looked dirty. "I was thinking of the pot. I remember the first time I saw it. Must've been about three. I'd been exploring Mum's wardrobe and there it was, a strange shiny thing almost hidden among a pile of boxes. I reached up to pull it out, but the boxes all came tumbling out too. I couldn't put the boxes back and I didn't want Mum to know I'd been touching her things."

Haras cringed at the memory of her mother coming into the room angry and yelling. She bit her lower lip as she remembered her mother tripping over the boxes on the floor. Holding her ankle, her mother had berated her, first for getting into her things and then for her twisted ankle. Now that same dread resurfaced at the most inconvenient times, as though it owned her. Haras frowned. Too many memories in the house.

Haras stood and shook herself. She didn't want that memory. "Well I need to get dressed." "What will we do for lunch?"

Ahsha pulled a face. "I don't mind. No more chocolates though "Not a good breakfast."

Haras forced herself to grin.

Ahsha walked over to the window. "What about a salad? Your garden's looking rather lush again."

"Yep." Haras stretched up. "I've started putting into practice some of what I'm learning at uni. Even cultivating a few edible weeds."

Ahsha screwed her face up. "Yuk. You can leave those out of *my* salad."

"Ha ha. You won't even know they're in it. Anyway, I must get dressed." Haras pointed in the direction of the garden. "If you change your mind, you know where the healthy food is."

Ahsha reached out for Haras's coffee mug. "I'll put these in the dishwasher."

"Thanks," Haras said as she headed for the bathroom.

She showered the tiredness away and smiled as she inhaled the rose shower gel. She dressed in a new knee-length jumpsuit and was admiring it in a mirror when she heard Ahsha humming outside. She followed the sound. "Like my new jumpsuit?"

"You could say it Jump-suits you." Ahsha said with a grin. "Hey I made a pun!"

Haras groaned. "Yeah, Right."

"I nearly bought a jumpsuit myself last week. Great for lounging around the house."

Haras laughed. "You must've read my mind. That's exactly what I bought mine for." She swung the empty basket she was carrying. "Now what greens shall we have?" She bent, picked a dandelion leaf and held it for Ahsha to see. "Good for the liver."

Ahsha watched and listened and tasted as Haras moved through her garden collecting flowers and greens for the salad.

Haras held up a clover leaf. "Trifolium looks good in a salad ..."

Ahsha puckered her lips. "You mean you can eat grass?"

"The leaves. Just a few. Let's add a few Nasturtium flowers for colour too." Haras ran her fingers along a dill stalk. "Try this."

Ahsha took the stalk and tried it. "Mmm, not bad. Aniseed." She looked at her watch. "How about a movie after lunch?"

"Sounds good to me. Anything in mind?"

"Romantic comedy?"

"Romance ... what did you say that intern of yours was like?" Haras waited and got the reaction she thought she would. Surprised delight.

"What? Who? Oh ..."

Haras poked her arm "No, No, just kidding. You should see your face, though."

Ahsha crossed her arms. "Hmm. Well you should see that wicked gleam in your eyes. That tells me you're definitely ready to date again, Haras Anona."

A slither of panic made Haras blink. She wasn't ready. Would she ever be ready? Did she want to be ready? She turned away. "Maybe I'll get a cat."

"What?" Ahsha pulled a face then bumped against Haras. "Soft and cuddly like ours?"

Haras grinned. "Always wanted one when I was little."

Ahsha nodded slowly. "Yeah, I think that's a good idea."

Haras sized up her basket of salad ingredients. "Well, if we get through this lot of vegies we'll be doing well."

Ahsha laughed and linked arms. "You think they might soak up some of the chocolate?"

Haras snorted. "I still have another box. Chocolates I mean. No. We'll have the movie for dessert."

They both laughed and went back inside for their afternoon meal and movie, which kept them both laughing all afternoon.

"Too much dessert!" Haras said and rubbed her stomach. "But it was begging me to eat it."

They both laughed again and Haras eased herself off the couch.

"Movie was good though," Ahsha said nodding her head as she took a lipstick and her phone from her handbag.

"Mmm, a bit corny. Too much starch."

Ahsha giggled. "But funny."

Using her phone camera as a mirror, she freshened up her lipstick. "Fancy some church to finish it off? Special service tonight. Starting early with finger food for tea."

Haras didn't. "Church? More food? No. I'm too full. Aren't you? I should do some dusting." She did have dusting to do. It was definitely not something she wanted to do, but removing the vase had made it obvious. The china cabinet needed going over.

Haras plonked herself back down on the couch and folded her arms over her sheer knitted top. It was new, a birthday present from Ahsha's mother. She crossed her legs and pressed her lips together. "You go, Ahsha."

"Are you sure? You might enjoy it. I do. I'll skip the finger food though."

Haras jiggled her foot back and forth nearly losing her slipper. "I know you do. Why do you bother asking? You know I *always* say no."

Ahsha scooped her bag up and looked directly into Ahsha's eyes. "One day you might just change your mind."

Haras diverted her gaze. "You'll be the first to know, I promise. Well … I take the promise bit back. I might not be able to keep it."

Ahsha smiled a pink lipstick smile that matched her bag. "Ok. Well, I'd better be going."

"Someone special at church?" Haras teased.

"Jesus," Ahsha said, and Haras laughed.

"Hope he appreciates how stunning you look in your new jeans!"

Ahsha put her hand on her heart. "It's what's in here that matters most."

"Well, chocolate is what I have in here," Haras said and placed her hand on her chest. She faked a moan at having eaten too many.

"Serves you right!" Ahsha giggled.

"Worth it!"

"See ya, Haras."

Haras opened the door for her. "Thanks for staying over. I needed your company today." She watched Ahsha nod and head for her car. It was a pristine as she was.

Haras closed the door and became acutely aware that the salad hadn't soaked up the chocolates. It was an effort getting her feet to go into the laundry for the duster, but they did.

"Some jobs are like that," she told herself. "You just have to start." She grabbed the duster by the handle and swirled the blue fibres. "One foot after another. That's how you do it. Come on."

Haras plodded over to the china cabinet. Maybe it was the house that made dusting so depressing. She inspected the hieroglyphics on the pot and wished her father had been there for her birthdays. What country had he and his parents moved to?

Since her mother's death Haras had tried to avoid thoughts about family, tried to fill the gap with work and study, but now she let all the unanswered questions race through her mind. Why had her mother had a change of heart about her finding her father? She'd been excited about something she'd found out just before the accident. What? A family secret? The more she allowed the questions to wander through her mind, the more curious she became.

Chapter

"Church was great." Ahsha said. "How was your dusting?"

Haras pressed the speaker button on her phone and put it on the computer desk. She turned a page of her textbook.

"Hard work. Harder than this horticulture assignment, but it's due on Wednesday. Gotta get it done." She finished typing the sentence while half listening to Ahsha.

"You got the speaker on? I can hear myself."

Haras stopped typing. "Yep. I'm multi-tasking."

"Oh well. Police Constable Ahsha here. Just checking up on you."

Haras smirked as one of Ahsha's renditions of a previous sermon jumped into her mind—a boy with a sling killing a giant. "Did you smite any giants tonight Constable Ahsha?"

"I did." Ahsha snickered. "I dusted a few off. Your duster would have fitted in well."

"Very funny. I'll remember to bring it with me if I ever decide to go to church."

Both girls laughed.

"Hey, tonight's sermon reminded me of your urn. It's empty like the tomb Jesus was buried in."

Haras blinked. "Urn? Of course! It's an urn!"

"What?"

Haras snapped her textbook shut. "Sorry Ahsha. I'll ring you back."

Urn? Ahsha had called the pot an urn. She'd found nothing searching online for her father, but what if she searched for urns? She saved her assignment and closed the file.

Her fingers hit the wrong keys, too slow for her thoughts. Ancient treasure. Urns. Egyptian. Her eyes opened wide. A site actually listed hieroglyphics, but were they the same as the ones on her pot?

She rushed into the kitchen, and returned with the pot. "Yes."

The hieroglyphics etched into her urn, were very similar to those listed on the website, but what did they mean? She did a search on translating hieroglyphics and could hardly believe what she found—a hieroglyphic typewriter!

She found the symbols on her pot, and wrote the English letter associated with each one. It translated as a puzzling sort of message. *Find the ancient path.* She tapped the desk with the tips of her fingernails and repeated the words.

What would her name look like? She couldn't resist it. H-A-R-A-S her fingers tapped without a typo. A picture of twisted flax followed by a vulture, a mouth, another vulture and folded cloth appeared.

"Ha!" *So that's what my name looks like!*

Haras frowned. "Vulture?" She didn't like the sound of that in her name. "Mouth?" Did her name mean something that was hungry? She pushed the thought away. She had work in the morning and Monday-itis wasn't an option, so she texted Ahsha and headed for bed.

Find the ancient path. Haras fell asleep thinking about it. She dreamed of urns and people, and whispering and secrets. When she woke the following morning, the words were still there. They continued to pop into her mind off and on throughout the day. She even upset one of her customers by calling the potted plant she was delivering an urn. The customer sympathized with her when she explained, but shook her head as Haras replaced the wilting leafy plant with the fresh new potted one. Haras imagined her thoughts, "Young people these days. What's the world coming too. Urns?"

Haras had to deliver a new flowering orchid to the medical centre where Ahsha worked. She was pleased for the opportunity to tell Ahsha in person about the incident with the customer. Ahsha's hand flew to her mouth preventing a laugh. She shook her head just like the customer had. "Find the ancient path. Maybe the words are significant."

Haras looked around. No doctors in sight. She leaned against the counter. "Maybe. It's beginning to feel that way only I wish it wouldn't come into my mind at the most inconvenient moments."

Ahsha began speaking into her headset. She waved at Haras and mouthed the word. "Lunch?"

Haras nodded and left, relieved she'd missed the new doctor. She wasn't looking for a date. She couldn't. She shook her head and changed the direction of her thoughts. She loved the freedom and variety of her job. Choosing flowers at the market, working with clients, delivering flower and plant arrangements, creating floral designs - it was a great job. Liberating. She especially loved chatting with clients.

Her boss believed in giving everyone a chance to find out what they liked doing. Haras knew she wasn't designed to answer phones. Ahsha seemed happy enough doing it. Filing - Haras hated that too. She didn't mind being on the computer. Her father had been a computer addict.

She knew that much about him. Her mother had told her often enough. They had that in common, but data entry? No way. She was a creative and her job left room for her to think, dream, and design. It left plenty of room for those words to nag her as well. Ancient path? It wasn't an unpleasant nag.

Over lunch Haras plied Ahsha with questions. "Where do you think the ancient path could be? Why would someone have it inscribed onto an urn? Do you think my father set off to find it? Maybe I'll find him if I find the ancient path. What do you think?" She didn't give Ahsha a chance to answer.

"How am I supposed to find my father and tell him how sorry Mum was?"

"Your salad's getting cold, Haras."

"What? Oh. Sorry." She laughed. "I am rabbiting on. Just as well it's not hot soup."

"Rabbit on some of your lunch. It's nearly time for me to go back to work."

"Hmm." Haras took a bite.

"I can see your thoughts churning. You're not with me today. That's two days in a row!"

Haras looked at her.

"Maybe you need to sort through your mother's things. Maybe there's something there that will help you find the answers, like a letter from your father or something. Anyway I've got to go." She left, and Haras finished her salad without even tasting it.

Haras finished her lunch and walked slowly back to her car. She was about to get in when a new display in the library window caught her eye. History. She stopped. Maybe they'd have something on ancient paths.

The librarian was helpful. She found a book on ancient paths.

Haras flipped through the pages.

… entrances to temple complexes … paths that the dead travelled on their way to eternal life … private roads … public roads … king's road … It spoke of literal paths and symbolic paths. She snapped it shut. If the ancient path wasn't a literal path, there was no point looking for it. It wouldn't help her find her father. She glanced at her watch. Now she was late for work. She'd have to stay late to make it up.

Later that evening Ahsha phoned and Haras grumbled. The library had only widened her search from physical to metaphorical paths.

"You were right. It is time to go through my mother's things."

Haras grimaced at the glee she heard in Ahsha's voice.

"Right? Again?"

Haras tapped her desk. "Yes, again! I've decided I'm going to take a few days off and sort through Mum's things."

"Good idea."

"I know. I'm full of them."

Haras pushed a curl of hair behind her ear. "I wish Mum hadn't changed the subject whenever I tried to talk about my father's side of the family. I wish I'd known them. What do you think the family secret could be?"

"You know I have no idea, but if you want me to come over, I'll help."

Haras turned the computer on. "Thanks, but it's a bit late, and I have an assignment to work on tonight."

"I didn't mean right now."

"Oh. Thanks, Ahsha."

Just the thought of going through her mother's things had been too much before, but now with a purpose, Haras was ready to face it.

Chapter 

Don't avoid it. Just start. Haras repeated the words each day and pushed herself to complete the sorting task, but it continued to loom over her bigger than her uni assignments had. Some things she sorted to keep and some to give away. Most of her mother's stuff went into a 'giving away' box, but she didn't find anything that could help. She was ready to give up. Perhaps she should just sell the house and everything in it.

She thought about the attic and knew she needed to check it out as well. Her mother had left some of Gran's stuff there.

She found her flashlight lantern and went into the laundry. The manhole to the attic was too high to reach by standing on a chair, so she got the ladder from the shed and climbed up.

There wasn't much in the attic, just three brown boxes, some equally brown looking cushions and the smell of years of untouched places. Haras dragged the boxes to the manhole, and then she knew why her mother had left them there. How was she going to get them down?

She opened one. It had a few old newspapers in it. She lifted each one out, shook it to make sure nothing was hidden inside, and piled them on the floor. The second box had a moth-eaten quilt, a few old glass vases that might be worth selling, and some old family photos. They needed closer inspection—in better light.

The third box contained old books. Dusty old books. Haras stretched and sneezed. She grabbed one of the cushions and flopped down onto it. Another gust of dust assailed her. She opened one book after another, read whatever inscriptions she found inside, and shook each book before placing it back into the empty newspaper box.

The last three books in the box didn't inspire hope. They looked like spy novels, not her mother's favourite genre. She picked one up and shook it. An old, yellowing envelope slipped out. The envelope had a vaguely familiar address on the back. She pulled out the contents - a painted sketch and a photo of the same house. Three people were standing in front of it. It had a grand front entrance that was somewhat familiar too.

Haras turned the photo over, "The photo you wanted - three of us like three of you. Love Deerg." She clenched her teeth, angry at her mother. She could have at least mentioned she had a photo of her father somewhere, even if she didn't know where. Haras relaxed as she remembered why the address was familiar. She'd visited it with her mother.

She climbed down the ladder and phoned Ahsha.

"Ahsha! I found a photo. We visited the house in the photo. I remember it. We went on a long drive. I kept pestering Mum." Haras mimicked the familiar question. "Are we there yet?"

They both said it a few times in unison.

"Anyway, we stopped outside this house." Haras looked at the photo. "A man was in the garden, pruning. I don't think he knew who we were. He kept pruning most of the time we were there."

Haras ran her finger over the front door in the photo, but couldn't remember what the man looked like. She did remember being hungry.

"We had our picnic lunch in the car. Mum told me the house had a grand entrance and belonged to my *grand* parents." Haras pressed her lips together in a tight frown. "Don't remember why we didn't go in. I wanted to, but mum made me stay in the car. She must've spoken to the gardener—can't remember."

"Maybe they had already moved. I'll come over. Stay the night if you like."

Haras paced the floor and rushed to open the door for Ahsha when she finally arrived. Before she had time to put her overnight bag down, Haras was showing her the envelope and contents.

"Deerg's mother?"

Haras nodded and ran her hand through her hair. "Same hair."

Ahsha giggled. "It would be if you hadn't dyed yours red. You do have the family likeness … tall and slender like your grandmother." Ahsha elbowed Haras. "You could be mistaken for her."

Haras did a quick twirl. "A younger version, of course." She stopped and took a deep breath.

"Grandmother. The word sounds so lovely." Haras pointed at the photo. "Look at the necklace she's wearing. I found one like it in Mum's things. I'll show you. It could be the same one."

Ahsha followed her into her mother's bedroom. "Wow. Look at all the boxes. You have been busy. Well done."

"Thanks."

A necklace lay on the oak dresser. In the centre was a circular, silver band with a stone heart hanging inside it. Haras ran her finger around the band. "I like antique silver. Not so keen on the heart."

"No. The heart doesn't quite fit. A bit too … I don't know."

Haras held the necklace to her neck and Ahsha fastened the catch. They faced the mirror.

She nodded at the photo. "Mmm. I'm definitely going to visit that house again."

Ahsha picked the envelope up. "32 Lessing Street, Wattyl. I'll come too, if you like."

Haras looked at her. "That would be great, but first I need some help getting a few things down from the attic. Feel like helping me with that?"

Ahsha did and they soon had everything sitting on the laundry bench as well as a trip planned.

Haras grinned. "Thanks." She clenched her fists and did a little victory dance. They were going to visit the house in the photo. That was a positive action towards finding her father, finding family.

Ahsha laughed. "Now that looks like the books aren't the only weight that's been lifted."

Haras stopped and patted her own back. "Yep. That's a load off my back!"

Chapter

"Everything okay?" Ahsha whispered as Haras expelled some of her nervousness with a deep breath.

Haras nodded and led the way up the steps. A few chipped edges stole every hint of grandness the entrance had once projected. She knocked on the hard wooden door of 32 Lessing Street, and listened. She could hear footsteps running towards them.

A young girl opened the door and stood in the doorway holding the brass knob.

"Hello."

Her rosebud smile and golden locks stole some of Haras's anxiety, helped by the air-conditioned breeze the girl let escape from inside.

"Who is it?" The sharpness of a man's voice brought some back.

"Two ladies, Grandpop."

An unshaven man appeared behind the little girl. He was bulging out of a grubby white singlet and grey shorts. He glared at them. "What do you want? We're not buying."

"We're not selling," Haras said. "My grandparents … Mr & Mrs Anona live here—or they used to. I just wanted to know if you know anything about them."

"Never heard of them. Grandparents? If they were your grandparents how come you don't know where they are?"

His gruff voice sent shivers down her back, but Haras stood her ground. She needed to know. She pulled the photo from her bag and held it up. Her hand shook a little.

"I only just found out they were my grandparents and I'm looking for them."

"Well they don't live here. We do. We've been here 'bout fifteen years, and I don't know 'em. My woman won't neither." The shook his head at the photo. The girl started sucking her thumb.

Haras's heart sank. She put the photo back in her shoulder bag. "Sorry for waking you."

The man muttered as he ran his fingers through his grey hair. "You woke me," he said as he disappeared back inside.

"Sorry, and thanks," Haras called after him.

The little girl waved before disappearing inside along with her Grandpop and the air-conditioned breeze. Haras and Ahsha waved back.

The next house was no better. Number 34 didn't know anyone. They'd just moved into the area. Haras and Ahsha turned to go.

"Two down." Haras waved a fly away. "And how many to go?"

"Deerg? You looking for Deerg?" A sun-wrinkled man called out to them as he leaned over his pruning shears.

Haras's mouth flew open. "What?" She stopped. Ahsha bumped into her.

"Couldn't help overhearing you." The man pulled at his cap and set it back over the few strands of wispy hair clinging to his head. "Had a few owners they have."

Haras and Ahsha looked at each other and then starred back at the man.

"Deerg? Yes. Deerg. Do you know him?" Haras reached into her bag for her photo as they walked towards the man. Haras turned the photo so the neighbour could see it over the hedge.

"Haven't seen Deerg for years though."

His bad dentistry was a bit off-putting.

"Yep, that's him and his family. Had a dog too. Stopped to chat he did, when he wasn't in a hurry - was mostly in a hurry."

Haras could hardly believe it. He knew her father? "Do you know where they went?"

He shook his head. "Long time ago. Memory's not that good."

Haras's hands shook as she put the photo back in her bag. She wanted to know everything he knew about her father.

The man removed his cap to wipe a row of sweat. "Long time ago. Wish I could remember more."

It wasn't that hot but Haras wished she had worn a hat. Ahsha had. It matched her top. Haras had been too preoccupied with typing the address into her GPS. Her hat was still sitting on a kitchen chair. She glanced at Ahsha. Ahsha was like a flower growing in the garden – a rather tall one, but just as quiet.

"Well, thanks. Anyone else around here who might know?" The neighbour, number 36 lifted his cap again and scratched his head. "Hang on. I think someone did mention something. Moving overseas - other side of the world somewhere. I'll ask around if you like."

"Thanks. If you hear anything, do you mind emailing me?" Haras reached into her bag for pen and paper."

"Yeah. Sure. Will get my son to help me. Not that good with computers. Eyes aren't what they used to be."

He was staring at Ahsha's wide brimmed raffia, cloche hat. Ahsha smiled under it.

"Do you think the neighbour on the other side will know anything more?" Haras asked.

"Couldn't say. Worth a try."

Haras gave the man her email address before they left and found herself smiling at Ahsha's hat too.

Ahsha pulled a face. "What? Why are you looking at my hat like that?"

"Wishing I had mine. I think the man liked it too."

"Yeah. He did. My Melbourne Cup hat." She tapped a matching pink fingernail against the brim and straightened her back. "I hope someone's home at Number 38."

Someone was, an elderly woman in a flouncy floral dress. Perhaps it was one she'd had since the fifties. Haras's nose automatically clamped shut as the cigarette smell assaulted her. The stale smell was such a contrast to the fresh dress. An equally incongruous image of the woman dancing popped into Haras's mind.

The woman flapped her spindly hand a few times, letting her bangle, jangle. Haras averted her eyes from the nicotine stained fingers and the veins that stood out over the parched skin on her arm.

"Saturday afternoon's a good time to be visiting. I'm always home Saturday afternoon," the woman said. "I dress for visitors."

Haras showed her the photo. "My grandparents used to live in this street. I'm trying to find them. My father's name was Deerg Anona."

The woman leaned forward. "Your grandparents?"

Her musky perfume didn't mask the cigarette smell. Haras wanted to step back, but the woman had such a sweet frail smile, Haras didn't want to offend her.

The woman peered at the photo through her glasses. "Yes, she does look like you."

"Haven't heard of Deerg since he left home. His parents moved overseas somewhere. I do know that. That must be ten years ago. No, more than ten. Could be getting on for eighteen years. My! Where did all those years go? Time goes so quickly. The years just zap away. The older you get the faster they go. Our children …"

Haras was more interested in finding out what the woman knew about Deerg. She wasn't interested in the lady's children. The woman pushed at her glasses.

"Don't know much, sorry. Never in each other's pocket. We all worked. Kept to ourselves. Too busy I guess." She looked at Ahsha. "Love your fancy pink hat."

"Thanks. It's my Melbourne Cup hat."

The woman nodded slowly. "I had a hat with little flowers like yours, once upon a time. Never been to Melbourne though, been to a few horse races though … long time ago." She looked at Haras and frowned. "It's a small town. Bound to be others around who remember your grandparents. Try some of the shops. How long are you staying?"

"Today. It's just a day trip. We thought we'd find out more than we have."

"Might take a bit of time. If you want somewhere to stay, I've a spare room." She nodded and Haras felt a twinge of sadness for the woman. She was probably lonely.

"That's very kind of you," Ahsha said.

Haras nodded. She had no intention of staying. "We'll keep that in mind. Well, we'd better keep going."

"Good luck with it. I hope you find what you're looking for."

"Thanks," both girls said together.

"Have a lovely Saturday," Asha said.

The woman smiled and Haras felt guilty. Asha's kind word had made the old woman beam and stand a little straighter. Haras forced a smile, but her heart was heavy and she felt irked.

The woman continued to stand at the door as they walked back down the drive. Haras glanced back. The woman was a frail, tired looking flower. Haras was tempted to run back and tell her she would visit her some time, but of course she knew she wouldn't. She waved and the flower perked up again.

The smile dropped as reality hit her. Haras grumped again. "Fancy knowing so little about your neighbours!"

"Haras!" Ahsha lowered her eyes and her voice. "She'll hear you."

Haras didn't care. The heat had stolen her compassion.

Ahsha straightened her hat. "Anyway, what do you know about your neighbours? I don't know ours. Do you know yours?"

Haras didn't know them all. She hadn't made the effort to visit the ones who'd just moved into the area. She shrugged and licked her lips. They were dry. "I need a drink. Let's have a break. Sit in the car for a bit before we do the other side of the road?"

"Sounds good to me." Ahsha titled her head back and peered at Haras. "You do look a bit bothered."

Haras frowned. There was a bite in the sun that sucked at her energy. Disappointment did too, and there were so many places she still needed to visit. How many shops were there? It would take more than a weekend to visit them all.

Ahsha sipped the last of her water and broke the silence as they sat in the car. "I'm still a little sick from travelling."

Haras gulped down her last mouthful of water and looked at her. "You do look a bit pale. More than usual. I'm glad I don't suffer from car sickness."

Mildly refreshed, they both headed across the road to Number 33. It turned out to be no better than the other side of the road. "Yes, the family in the photo did live there," but "No. They don't anymore."

They tried all the houses on that side of the street, right down to the corner, Number 67. Those who were home and had known Deerg, which weren't that many, hadn't heard of him since he left home. They thought his parents had immigrated, maybe to the other side of the world. No-one could remember much. Each person suggested some other place Haras could try, and her shoulders began to sag under the weight of them all. It would take forever to visit them.

"One brick wall after another!" Haras pouted. She folded her arms and pressed them against her chest. She let the dark thoughts harass her.

Ahsha plopped her hat on Haras's head. "You are just hot and disappointed. Too much sun. Maybe we should call it a day."

Haras unfolded her arms. "You're right."

Ahsha grinned. "Again?"

Haras managed a weak smile. She shook her head and waved at the man from Number 36 as they drove passed.

"It'll take days to visit all the places everyone's suggested. Let's get a bite to eat before we head home. We can show the photo and ask if anyone knows them."

Chapter F

"For goodness sake Haras."

"What?" Haras blinked and braked.

Ahsha clutched the dashboard. "You're speeding!"

Haras glanced at the speedo. "Whoops. Sorry, I was miles away."

Another fifteen minutes and she was *miles away* again. What if she took a holiday? She could go back and keep looking. But what if she found their next address? What then? She didn't have enough money or paid leave to keep taking holidays.

"Haras!"

"I know." Haras checked the speedo and slowed down again.

How could she get enough money to keep looking? Sell her house? But what about her garden? She had it just how she wanted it. And what about her studies? Haras licked her lips. What if she rented her house out? That would give her an income while she searched.

Haras arched her neck. "Yes!" That would work. The money from the rent could pay for her to stay in Wattyl. That way she could begin searching in earnest. She could finish her studies after she found them. She glanced at Ahsha."What? I missed that. Did you want to stop?"

Ahsha pulled her hair into a pony-tail, wiped her neck and let her hair drop. "We just passed a truck-stop. Let's go back. I'm hungry."

Haras agreed. It was time for a break. She slowed down and headed back. Her mind didn't stop racing with possibilities as they ate the burgers they bought and sipped their coffee. She didn't tell Ahsha what she was thinking. She felt sure Ahsha would try to discourage her. She needed time to think it through anyway.

They drove in silence most of the way home. Ahsha slept, and Haras wished she had cruise control to keep herself from speeding.

By the following weekend Haras had made up her mind. Renting would not only give her an income, but it would get her away from the house with all its memories that kept dragging her down. She invited Ahsha over and told her what she planned to do.

Ahsha put her teacup down a little too forcefully. The tea spilled into the white china saucer. "Everything? You want to leave your job and everything? What about your studies?"

Her words annoyed Haras. She was right. Ahsha was trying to discourage her from moving. "I don't have any leave left. If I don't get out, I think I'll suffocate. I feel so frustrated." Haras clenched her fists. "Everything here reminds me I have no family, and I've got to find my father. I've just got to find him and tell him what Mum said."

Ahsha played with a long strand of her hair. "Don't I count for anything? We're family, aren't we? We try to be."

Haras bit down on her thumbnail.

Ahsha continued. "Surely our friendship isn't suffocating? We have a lot of fun together … don't we?"

Haras put her hand on Ahsha's arm. "I don't mean you, Ahsha. I didn't mean it like that. You're not suffocating me, and we do have a lot of fun together and your mother is lovely. I will miss you all terribly."

Ahsha continued looking down. "You won't know anyone there. Just go for the weekend. I'll come with you if you like. What if …?"

Haras stood up and paced across the room and back. She felt agitated and could see Ahsha was too. She'd never seen Ahsha as agitated as this, but it was no use. Haras couldn't see any other way. Nothing was going to stop her from looking for her father. She had made up her mind. She wasn't going to be afraid of going alone to a new place. She wasn't.

Haras sat down again, and took a deep breath. "It's scary, but we can phone each other."

Ahsha pouted. "I know I should be more encouraging. I know how important your mother's words are and knowing your roots is important too. I just don't want you to be a long-distance friend."

Haras felt herself wavering.

Ahsha batted her eyelids. "Won't you change your mind? Pretty please?"

Haras couldn't help laughing. She shook her head. "Pretty no. It's only five hours away." Haras looked into her cup and wished she'd made a mug of coffee. Her lips were dry. What if they really had moved to the other side of the world? What if ... She needed a refill. Ahsha's what-if's were catching. "You can catch a bus and come visit me. Want a refill?"

Ahsha leaned on one elbow spreading her manicured fingers over her mouth. "No. Mine's okay, and the bus would take all day to get there." She brushed a stray hair from her eyes and frowned again. "I hate travelling. Every family holiday I ended up being car-sick." She followed Haras into the kitchen. "You know I'm a homebody. I love it at home, and you're the best friend I've ever had."

Haras placed her cup under the coffee machine nozzle and put in a new capsule. "Thanks Ahsha. You're the best, too."

Ahsha pursed her lips. "You're never jealous or catty, like other girls. I won't have anyone to go out with. Your home is like an heirloom, isn't it? Didn't you inherit it from your mother and didn't she inherit it from her mother?"

"I'm not selling the house, Ahsha. I just plan to rent it out."

"Renting is risky, Haras. What if the tenants wreck your home, and what about your garden?" Ahsha pointed out the window. "You have it all planted the way you want it. You're nearly self-sufficient."

"Ahsha, you know there are insurance policies for landlords. Anyway, if I lose all this, it will be an opportunity in disguise. It would be fun to redesign the house put my stamp on the place."

Haras topped her coffee with frothy milk and sprinkled it with shaved chocolate topping. She would do what she had in mind to do and nothing was going to stop her. She would make an appointment with a real estate agent and get the house ready to rent.

"I just *have* to find my father, Ahsha. Mum wouldn't have said I must, if it wasn't really important. I feel kinda empty and I'm sure it's because I don't know him."

Ahsha said nothing, so Haras poked her. "You will help me, won't you?"

Ahsha poked her back. "You know I will, but I don't want to help you go away."

"I'm not going tomorrow. I'll finish the semester at uni first. It will take a while to get rid of stuff and pack everything. I'm only going to take what I can carry on my back."

Ahsha looked at her phone and gasped. "Oh no! I'm late."

"Late?"

"Oh rats! I've missed it now. I had a pedicure booked for eleven-thirty and its eleven-thirty already. I'd better call them and reschedule."

Ahsha stood and paced the room with her phone at her ear. She apologized and made a new pedicure booking. When she'd finished, Haras stood up. "Now that you have some time, do you want to stay and help? No time like the present."

"Not really, but I will have another coffee now."

They wandered through the house with their coffee, making plans about what to keep and what to sell. Haras opened the door to what had been her mother's room and they looked around.

It seemed like a shell without her mother's stuff. She was glad the boxes had gone. One less thing to do.

"What's the urn doing there?" Ahsha asked pointing to the open bedroom window. She put her coffee down and moved the urn from the sill to the bedside table. "It might fall out the window."

Haras stood for a moment looking at the urn. "I suppose so. The phone rang so I put it there and forgot about it." She frowned. "Mum couldn't bear to look at that pot. She said, Deerg wanted it back when they broke up, but she hid it from him and wouldn't give it back. I heard her telling someone. I wish she hadn't gone on and on about not being a part of Deerg's story any more. Sometimes it makes me so angry. Like now!" Haras gritted her teeth. "Mum said she wasn't interested in what *he* treasured, and didn't know where his pot was." Haras scratched the back of her head. She hadn't meant to blurt all that out.

Ahsha gathered her blonde hair into a ponytail then let it drop. "People say things like that when they're upset. They try and justify their position. She probably didn't mean it like it sounded."

Haras closed the window. "I don't hear your parents saying things like that."

"No, not now. But it was rough to start with. They were both so angry, before the divorce. Things didn't settle down until Mum became a Christian."

Ahsha patted an old recliner. "… and don't forget to check the back of the couch before you sell it. I always find money in Dad's when I visit him. It slips from his pocket. He used to call it my pocket money." Ahsha smiled. "Sometimes I think he put money there for me to find."

Haras put her hand down the back of the recliner. It felt crumbly. She'd hardly ever come in to vaccum her mother's room, let alone the recliner. "Can't feel much, but it needs a vacuum."

"Not like that." Ahsha said as she pulled the recliner away from the wall and undid the bottom flap at the back. A pile of dusty crumbly stuff fell out. She picked up two coins and an earring and placed them on the dresser.

"Yuk. I never knew you could do that."

"I'll get the vacuum cleaner," Haras said.

Haras returned and vacuumed the rest. "We might as well do the ones in the lounge after this."

"I can't believe you never knew about undoing the flap."

"Doesn't look like Mum knew either. That was a lot of …" Haras pulled a face. "… who knows what?"

Ahsha held out a handful of crumpled wrappers. "She liked chocolate."

Haras laughed. "Those wrappers look more like mine. In fact, I remember eating that one."

Ahsha flapped the wrappers at Haras. "Back in the olden days when you were three?"

They laughed and went back into the lounge to look for more vintage chocolate wrappers.

"Never know, you might find a chocolate still in a wrapper," Ahsha said pretending one of the wrappers held a chocolate.

Haras laughed. "That reminds me of Mum's favourite story. When I was about two, I came into the house eating a lolly. Mum asked me where I got it. I told her I found it on the footpath. She told me to spit it out. She said it was dirty. I told her it wasn't. I had licked it clean."

"Yuk!" They both laughed again, and when Ahsha found a half-eaten dried-up chocolate bar and held it out for Haras to lick clean.

Haras bulked. "You first!" That set them off and they laughed so much they couldn't stop.

"What's this?" Ahsha said as she pulled out a yellowing piece of paper tucked up inside the recliner. She unfolded the paper and began to read. Haras leaned over her shoulder.

We kept it a secret from Elle until her doll broke. There was a silver necklace inside wrapped in a handkerchief with the words Little Lamb embroidered on it. She often sang a song about a little lamb. When she first came she said her sister sang it with her. She soon forgot that. I let her believe I was her mother. But when she asked about the things in the doll, I had to tell her the truth. I wasn't her birth mother and now she's gone.

Haras took the paper and turned the page over. No name. No date.

"Who's Elle?" Ahsha asked.

Haras re-read the first sentence. "Don't know. I think it might be my grandmother's name. We never talked about her. I never met her, but it sounds kinda familiar, like it could be."

"You've got a silver necklace, like the one the lady in the photo was wearing."

"Yeah."

"Maybe it's the one in this letter. Your grandmother's name could be Elle. If she was adopted that would explain the lack of relatives."

"It could. Don't know." Haras shook her head. "No. This letter could be about anyone. I mean, maybe one of mum's friends. I don't know." She ran her fingers through her hair.

"But a silver necklace Haras? It would be vintage by now, like yours."

Haras looked at her eager face, took a quick breath and listened.

"Didn't you say you had a text from your mother saying she had some exciting news to share with you, and you never got to hear what it was?"

Haras shrugged. "Don't remind me. It's so frustrating. I suppose this letter could've had something to do with it. Guess we'll never know." She pointed to the letter. "That Elle's gone, my father has, and so has mum." Haras pressed her fingers into her eyes, then rubbed them.

Ahsha put her arm around Haras's shoulder.

"I'm sorry. I shouldn't have brought it up."

Haras shook her head. She wasn't going to think about her mother. She wasn't going to cry. She didn't. She stared at the letter. Was it, could it be a link to her father?

Chapter 9

Giants! Every problem was like a giant looming up before her, or maybe a mountain. There were so many things to do. What should she do with all her personal stuff, the things she didn't want to throw out, like her photo albums? She couldn't carry them on her back and she wanted to travel light. She wanted to be free to go wherever she had to, in order to find her family. The only thing she would have to make room for was her urn. She just couldn't leave that behind. She wanted to give it back to her father.

Find the ancient path. The words caught her off guard. Haras had tried logic to get rid of the idea of looking for one, but the message was urging her on again. Illogical as it seemed she couldn't shift the idea that if she found that path, she'd find her father.

"No problem," Ahsha's mother said when she found out what was bothering Haras. Their house had plenty of storage space and Haras was welcome to store her stuff with them.

Haras was pleased they were such good friends. Without their practical help she knew she would never be able to get the house ready for the tenants.

From time to time, Ahsha tried to talk her out of going and Haras began to doubt that she was doing the best thing, but it was too late to change her mind. She had started down this path and couldn't see any other way to do what her mother had wanted her to do. She'd thought about it long enough. It was time to act.

Finally, Haras was ready to leave, but she could tell Ahsha wasn't ready for her to go. Still, she said her promised, 'not-forever' goodbyes. She had a long drive ahead to the backpacker's hostel. It wasn't far from where her grandparents had lived, but it was a long way from where Ahsha was standing.

Haras hugged her. "Mmm you smell like roses. I'm tempted to put you in the car to freshen it up."

Ahsha didn't even smile. She held on and Haras almost weakened her resolve not to stay, but she didn't. She couldn't. It was too late.

"You're still my best friend Ahsha. We've got our phones."

"Goodbye," Ahsha whispered.

Haras hugged her again. She didn't want to say goodbye. It was too definite.

"It's not really goodbye. I'll see you soon. You'll see."

Haras patted Ahsha'a arm and got into the car. Despite the enthusiasm she projected, there was a knot in her stomach. Maybe Ahsha was right. Maybe she should be just going for the weekend. She let the window down a little for a breath of fresh air.

Haras pulled into the service station for petrol and a snack and pushed the anxious thoughts away. Her thoughts were skidding all over the place and she needed to calm down.

She drove past a shop selling war memorabilia and could almost smell its musty past. Her thoughts returned to family. The last war had broken up many family lines, hers included. It had left her gran and pop with no other family and no desire to talk about the past.

She tapped the steering wheel as she remembered how uncomfortable her gran had been whenever war was mentioned. It wasn't politics, sex or religion that one had to avoid talking to them about, it was *The War*. Talking about religion was her mother's taboo though. That was odd. Well, she wasn't like her mother. She put up with Ahsha's religious talk. Well, sometimes.

Four and a half hours later Haras parked her car at the hostel. She was glad she'd paid extra for a single room. She didn't want company. She didn't want to worry about keeping her things safe, either. It had been a long day and she was ready for a good night's sleep, not the sound of others snoring.

It wasn't snoring that interrupted her sleep. It was occasional bouts of wind and rain rattling the sash window. She didn't like it. It reminded her of the stormy weekend of her mother's car accident. On that terrible weekend, her whole life had changed. Thunder and lightning had woken her then as well. It was probably the only thing that would have. The doorbell hadn't. She'd slept through that, recovering from her eighteenth birthday celebrations. Haras didn't want to remember it. She pulled the bed covers up over her head and willed herself to sleep.

It was still raining the following morning when Haras got up. She brushed her hair and thought about the necklace in the photo. She was sure it was the same one she'd found in her mother's things. She was glad she'd brought it with her. It would look good with the multi-coloured, striped, v-neck top, she was wearing. The dark silver matched the grey stipe. It didn't look too bad with her love bracelet, even though it was shiny. They were both silver at least. Someone might even recognize the necklace, if it had been her grandmother's.

Her reflection in the mirror predicted the beginning of a new chapter in her life. She smiled.

You may never find your father or your grandparents.

Haras pushed the thought away. The necklace looked great! So did her new long lasting lipstick, not as pink as Asha's favourite colour. It too matched one of the stripes in her top.

"I can do this and I *am* doing this." Her reflection nodded. First stop the supermarket. There was one in the mall, according to the receptionist.

It was too stormy for a walk, so she took the car. The rain was still pelting down when she drove into the car park. She opened the door a little, pushed open her umbrella, climbed out, grabbed her bag, pushed the door shut and ran. Thunder punched right into her heart. Haras lifted her umbrella to see where she was going. Too late! She heard and felt the shock of someone's spongy body as they collided.

"Sorry!" Haras gasped as the contents of the elderly woman's bag spilled out. She bent to help the woman gather her things and apologized again. With each grocery item she grabbed, Haras fumed. The umbrella wasn't big enough. Her cotton top was stuck to her back. She shivered. The woman didn't even seem to be upset about her groceries. Her pale blue eyes were so calm, almost smiling. Finally, the last item was back in the bag and Haras and the woman headed for cover.

Haras shook her umbrella and pressed the down button. She squeezed the water from the ends of her hair and stopped to watch the woman. She'd placed her bags on the pavement and was wiping her hands with a flowery, blue, silk handkerchief, that matched her eyes. She patted at her thinning white hair, and Haras felt awkward. What should she say?

The woman stopped too. Her eyes widened. "You look just like a lady I once knew."

"Really!" The words jumped from Haras's mouth, rude, even to her own ears. She was hungry, it was raining and now she was wet. She didn't want to talk to this stranger. She felt bad, but her feet were rocks and her legs wobbly.

The woman continued talking, and when she mentioned her friend's name, Haras's ears pricked up. "Elle?" Now Haras was starring too. She wiped her damp hands on the front of her jeans and fumbled for the photo in her wallet.

The woman looked at it and nodded. "Elle."

Haras stared at her. "It is?" She couldn't believe it. "Are you sure?" Haras hoped the woman hadn't noticed her attitude.

"Yes, yes. That's Elle." She looked at Haras. "You look just like her."

"My father's name is Deerg Anona."

The woman's mouth remained open, then became a broad smile as she held out her hand. "Mine's Emme."

Haras freed up her right hand, nearly dropping her wallet, and shook Emme's.

"Yes, Elle's son was called Deerg. Can't say I'd recognise him though."

Haras turned the photo over and Emme read the words.

"The photo you wanted - three of us like three of you. Love Deerg." Emme nodded slowly. "Yes she did only have one child."

Haras told her about the neighbours she'd visited and how few had really known them.

"Well that's not a surprise. Deerg was away at school. Not around as long as Elle and her husband. Many people knew Elle. Small town … mind you the years do zap away. I guess memories fade just as quickly. New people come and old ones can soon be forgotten. I've outlived my brother and my sister … and some of my friends."

Haras put her photo away. "I'm trying to find my father, Elle's son. You say you knew Elle? Do you have time for coffee?" She hoped the woman did.

The woman's eyes twinkled. There was so much light in them. "I do. There's a nice café in the mall." She pointed in the general direction.

"Here, let me carry your groceries," Haras said and Emme smiled again and handed her a bag.

At the café, Emme told the waiter Haras was the granddaughter of an old friend who'd been well-known in the area for her green thumbs.

"People loved Elle's witty gardening articles," Emme said. "Had a regular column in the local paper, she did. Collected and propagated rare orchids as well." Emme chuckled. "She gave me one, but it didn't last long under my care." She held up two plump hands as if that would explain it. "We often came into this mall for coffee, when it was first built—."

"Let me get you a towel," the waiter said. "You're both quite wet."

They were, and they welcomed the towel. The waiter took their orders and Emme insisted on paying, saying it was her work to do so. Haras couldn't understand how anyone could think such a thing.

Emme was looking at her necklace. "That necklace looks familiar."

Haras pulled it out. "I think it's the same one in the photo I showed you. It belonged to my mother. She did say it had been my grandmother's, but I thought she had meant her mother."

"Ah, Elle found one … yes, it does look like the one she found hidden inside her doll, when it broke." She pointed at the heart. "Yes, yes, I do remember. That's the stone she found at the beach."

Haras was speechless. The last of her doubts about the photo and the necklace were swept away. The photo was a family photo, *her* family photo, and Elle *was* Deerg's mother's name. She must have been the Elle in the letter.

Emme looked up and waved. She was looking at an elderly woman with thick braided, chalk-white hair. "Ollo, come and met Elle's granddaughter."

Ollo raised a thick white eyebrow and parked her sturdy body on the chair beside them "Well, well. Didn't know she had one. What a surprise!"

She didn't order a coffee. "Can't stay long," she said. She wanted to know everything. "Yes, Elle was well know. Must've had a cutting from every garden in town."

Ollo accentuated her r's with an accent Haras didn't recognise.

"The town was smaller den of course." She slapped her knee. "Us oldies still remember her."

Emme and Ollo exchanged nods.

"She must've won something every year at the flower-show," Emme said.

Do you know if Elle was adopted or not?" Haras asked.

"I did know dat," Ollo said. She turned to Emme. "Remember I told you."

Emme nodded. "Hmm. I think you did."

There was an air of authority in Ollo's voice that caused Haras to tense up. "She went off in search of birth family. I told you dat." Ollo frowned. "Well, can't stay and chat today. Doctors appointment."

After Ollo left, Emme leaned forward. "Ollo is Finnish. She came here with her mother after the war."

Emme continued chatting away until they finished their coffee. Her smiley conversation cheered Haras up. Emme was the happiest person she had ever met.

"If you find Elle, give her my new address," Emme said. "I'm in a retirement village now, so is Ollo."

"I'm at the Backpackers Hostel," Haras said. "The only one in town."

Haras tapped Emme's contact details into her phone and wrote down her own details on a small notepad for Emme.

Emme glanced at the notepaper. "Oh, I just had a thought. Why not visit the retirement village? Someone else might know more than I do. We have a happy hour on Friday's at five."

Haras nodded. "Okay. I will. Thanks."

"Even if you don't find her, keep in touch. I would love to hear about your journey. There's a whole world out there to explore! Don't let fear dictate what you will or won't do. You can go where you've never gone before and maybe you will find family on the way. If not, enjoy the journey."

With those words, the horizon before Haras expanded and she knew she'd made the right decision. She marvelled. She was like her grandmother, even following in her footsteps!

"It's such an amazing coincidence bumping into you like I did," Haras said.

Emme leaned forward and patted her arm. Her eyes overflowed with laughter, creating soft wrinkles in her rosy face.

"I call them God incidences. It's a sign that God is looking out for you, Haras."

Haras didn't want to argue. She stopped listening. Emme didn't seem to notice. Her eyes were pools of innocent happiness.

"I heard about an amazing lady … been walking around Europe."

Haras tuned in again.

"God keeps her safe and provides everything she needs."

Haras didn't want to listen to any God talk. She was still damp. It was time to go. She'd almost forgotten the reason for her trip to the mall. Maybe she was like her mother after all, when it came to religious talk. She didn't need a god to provide for her. She had the rent money, but there was something comforting in Emme's words. They assured her she was on the right path.

Chapter 11

Haras followed the GPS to the retirement village. She parked next to a red sports car and spotted Emme and Ollo.

"Nice car," Haras said.

Ollo didn't smile. "If you like that sort of thing," she said.

"It's a hire car," Emme said. "The young driver visits her grandfather from time to time."

"Oh. It doesn't look like a hire car."

"Come on then. Everyone's waiting to meet you Haras. Some remember Elle."

Haras stood looking at the car a moment longer, then let Emme lead the way inside.

A group of residents sat around in a mix of leather lounge chairs and old wood dining chairs, eating and drinking. Haras eyed the large stainless steel tray of nibbles and was suddenly hungry.

"Help yourself, Haras," Emme said.

Haras did. She put a sausage roll and barbequed chicken on a plate and followed Ollo to some empty seats. Before she could sit, Emme clapped her hands to get everyone's attention.

"I'd like to introduce our visitor. This is Haras, the young girl I told you about. She's looking for her family." Everyone clapped, some nodded.

Haras turned to Emme. "Thank you Emme for inviting me, and thank you everyone for agreeing to let me come today. As Emme said, I want to find out as much as I can about my family." She held up her photo and walked around the room showing it to everyone.

"Yes that's Elle Anona, alright," they agreed. Not many knew her husband or Deerg.

Ollo leaned towards Haras. "What would you like to drink, Haras?"

Haras glanced at the bottles. "The white wine, thanks."

A short, thickset man with a protruding belly waved his walking stick from across the room. "I know a little," he said. He was standing still, feet apart, but slowly approached Haras, when she looked in his direction.

Ollo went to get Haras a wine and the man held out his free hand.

"Names, Gereg."

Haras shook it and Gereg spaced his feet apart and leaned with both hands on his stick.

"Last I heard Elle was in Y'kahs, visiting her son." He tapped his walking stick on the carpet.

A woman interjected pointing to Gereg. "He always had an eye for her, he did."

Gereg shuffled his feet and tapped his walking stick on the carpet again. "Elle was a looker. Anna, my late wife corresponded with her a few times. She told me Elle found out she'd been adopted, and went looking for her birth family – a sister. I think she said something about an older sister. I still have the last postcard from her … sent to my Anna, of course."

"Of course!" a few chortled.

"I tried writing to her in Y'kahs to let her know my Anna had passed away, but my letters were returned." He tapped his stick again. "Didn't know her husband well … a quiet man." He looked intently at Haras. "I can see the family likeness. Wait here. I'll go and get the postcard. Left it on the table."

Ollo returned with a glass of wine and Haras nibbled on her chicken.

"Here," Ollo said. She placed a few paper napkins on the table and gave one to Haras.

Haras licked her fingers before wiping them. "Thanks, Ollo."

Gereg was soon back. His gait was as sad as his face, and he was panting heavily. He held out the postcard and his returned letter. "Give this to her if you find her."

Haras took a deep breath. "I will. Thank you." She turned the postcard over and held her breath. Elle had met up with her son Deerg in Y'kahs. They had all been there together. The address was still clearly visible. Haras wanted to catch a plane that very minute and find them.

She looked at the address on the returned letter and immediately her newfound hope dissolved. It had been returned. Did that mean they'd moved on?

The happy hour was soon over, but Haras continued chatting for a while, building up a picture of her grandmother. When they heard Haras speak about her horticultural studies, they all agreed she must've inherited that interest from Elle. Haras glowed.

As each one left they wished her all the luck in the world with finding her family and some wanted her to write back and let them know what she discovered.

Haras returned to the hostel and searched the internet for information about Y'kahs. It was on the other side of the world, nearly thirteen thousand kilometres away. A section on plants caught her interest, and she made a mental note about the edible plants that grew there. She decided she would go, even though it was so far away. But would her grandparents and father still be living there? The letter had been returned.

She sent a quick text message to Ahsha asking her to come for the weekend. She had some amazing news she wanted to tell her. It had all happened just as she wanted it to. She'd found some people who knew her father's parents, and she had an address, and the Elle in the letter was her grandmother, wow, and … she wouldn't be so pleased about the last bit of news … she was going to fly to the other side of the world, and … She had so much to tell her.

The weekend arrived and Haras waited for Ahsha at the bus station. Although Ahsha had her driving licence, she often said she was in no hurry to buy a car. She didn't need one for work or the weekends.

Haras was glad Ahsha had pushed herself to make the trip. As she stepped off the bus, bag in one hand and a ribboned chocolate box in the other, Haras thought she looked like a model about to walk the red carpet, except for the chocolates - their favourite, chocolate liqueurs. She felt a twinge of pride. This gorgeous creature, holding chocolates, was her friend, her best friend. For a moment, she wanted to forget about leaving. She wanted to go back home.

"I miss you already Ahsha," she said.

Ahsha grinned at her. "Aw, thanks. Me too." Neither spoke for a while, but as they drove back to the hostel, Haras couldn't contain her news. The whole story tumbled from her mouth.

Ahsha leaned forward when Haras told her about the amazing *coincidence.*

"Emme called it a *God incident, a sign.*" Haras waited for Ahsha's reaction.

"That sounds like a miracle to me," Ahsha laughed. "It's an answer to prayer. I've been praying you'd find your birth family. I prayed you'd bump into someone, but I never meant it literally!" Ahsha was beaming. "That's so amazing!"

"I thought that would make you happy." Haras grinned, but unexpectedly, some of Ahsha's awe rubbed off on her. "And that's not all. Emme recognised the lady in the photo. Her name's Elle! Elle, you know, the Elle in the letter, and she *is* my grandmother."

Haras parked the car and turned to face Ahsha. "Anna, one of the retirement village residents, got a postcard from Elle when they first moved to Y'kahs. Y'kahs is where they went. Her husband found it and gave it to me. Elle mentions meeting up with her son Deerg. Her son! She is my grandmother, Ahsha. She is!" Haras nodded vigorously. "Apparently I look just like her. We even have the same interest in gardening. Emme recognised the necklace too. And guess what?" Haras paused to grab a breath. "She was adopted. Emme's friend Ollo said so, and Anna apparently told her husband so too, when she was alive."

"Wow! That's ..." Before Ahsha could finish the sentence Haras continued.

"No-one knew what happened after that. But I have the address. Now I know where to go next. Y'kahs." She nodded again.

"Wow ..." Ahsha said and became silent as Haras continued telling her everything she had learned and planned to do.

Haras patted Ahsha arm. "I'm going to Y'kahs." She sat quietly letting the words sink in. They did and Ahsha reacted the way Haras thought she might.

"Y'kahs? Of all the places to go to! It's so far away."

Haras knew she had pushed Ahsha's fear buttons, but didn't expect to get an earful of them.

"It's not safe there."

Haras felt sorry for her. "Come on Ahsha. It's never that bad. It's easier to travel when you're young and its time I did some. It's an adventure, whatever the outcome." She was worried enough without Ahsha weighing her down with her concerns.

They didn't speak as they walked into the Hostel and up to the twin room Haras had booked for the weekend.

"Coffee?"

Ahsha flopped into the only arm-chair in the room and let her bag slip onto the floor. "Thanks. I could drink a gallon of it. I still have some motion-sickness from the bus trip. It was so long, but it did give me time to think. I realized, you leaving triggered the same kind of feelings I had when my father left, and the sermon this week was about fear and anxiety! *Full-grown love throws fear outside.* Well, I've been growing discouragement and fear instead of throwing it out." Ahsha took a sip of the coffee Haras gave her. "I'm sorry."

Haras swallowed. "That's okay. It's hard for me too."

"But Y'kahs, Haras! That's so far."

Haras sat down and stared into her small coffee cup. "I have to try."

They drank in silence.

"You want another coffee?" Haras asked as she finished hers. "I'm not used to small cups."

"No, thanks. I was exaggerating. I'm water-logged."

"Bathroom's down the hall."

"Thanks." Ahsha stood, stared at the carpet for a moment, then sighed. "I know you must look for your father. God spoke to me about that, too. It's the *reality that liberates*. I've always got God as my friend, and as you said, we do have our phones. Be back in a minute." She was.

Ahsha phoned her mother and her father and told them Haras's news. They both wanted to talk to Haras and both wished her well on her journey. They would miss her they said.

The weekend just zapped away from them after that. Haras and Ahsha spent the weekend watching movies and shopping. Mostly window-shopping for Haras - she was travelling light. Shopping for Ahsha - she wasn't.

In no time they were back at the bus station waiting. The moisture in Ahsha's eyes was threatening her make-up. Haras gave her a small box that contained some earrings she'd bought as a farewell gift.

"Wow. Thanks, Haras. I love them."

Ahsha handed Haras a fat envelope. "This is from mum, dad and me. We love you," she whispered and hugged her goodbye.

"Love you too. Thanks, so much. You didn't have to do this."

Haras waved and waited until the bus departed before opening the envelope. She gasped, dumbfounded. One hundred dollar notes were bulging out the end of a card. She counted them. Ten. Tears pricked her eyes. She could hardly see the words written in the card — *A blessing for your journey.*

Haras fumbled for a hanky, but couldn't find one.

Chapter

Inside the plane, Haras buckled herself in and felt more contented than she had been for a long time. She hoped whoever sat next to her was trustworthy and pleasant–that was one of the reasons why she'd paid the extra to go business class. She was glad of the extra leg space as well. The thousand dollars she'd been given was well spent.

A young woman of Asian appearance stopped beside her. Haras guessed she was probably in her mid-twenties. As the girl lifted her bag into the overhead compartment, she caught a whiff of oceanic perfume, but couldn't place it. She did recognize the distinctive brown patterned Louis Vuitton cabin bag and matching bracelet though. Ahsha had pointed one out to her, on one of their shopping trips. It was neither the style nor the price tag Haras had been looking for back then.

Her fellow passenger gathered her long black hair behind her before sitting down. Haras had never seen such long hair before. It came down below her tiny waist.

"Hi!"

"Hi. Your hair's amazing!"

The girl gave a half laugh. Her diamond earrings sparkled as she turned her head. "Thank you."

She clicked her seat belt together over her business suit. "Do you travel often?"

"No. This is my first long trip. You?"

"Yes. I do a lot of travelling, especially to Y'kahs. An old school friend of mine lives there. His sister's getting married and he asked me to partner him. And you?"

"I'm looking for family. Y'kahs was the last address I have for my grandparents."

"I hope you find them. What's their name?"

"Deerg Anona's my father's name. My grandmother's name was Elle."

"I'm Izzi. I'm staying at the Intent Hotel."

"Mine's Haras. I'm booked in at a backpacker's Hotel. Ata. I think that's how you pronounce it." Izzi nodded and ended the conversation by taking out the flight magazine.

Haras took a deep breath and exhaled slowly. She was finally able to relax for the flight.

As the plane soared above the clouds, a few air pockets made her stomach drop. They stole some of her contentment. She tightened her safety belt and hoped it wasn't a bad omen.

Long as the flight to Y'kahs was, it didn't tire Haras as much as she thought it would. The few bumps only temporarily snatched her carefree cover up, the company was pleasant and the flight uneventful. She'd even managed to get some sleep.

Haras cleared customs and took a taxi to the Ata hotel. She was soon enjoying the cool and quiet of her single room.

She made a call to Ahsha to let her know she was safe. Ahsha was glad to hear it, but she couldn't talk long. It was mid-morning and she was at work.

"But guess what," Ahsha said. "It just so happens that the girl who's filling in for you at work is planning a family. She's thinking of baby names and their meanings already, and guess what name she's chosen for a girl?"

"I give up. What?"

"Emme!"

"You are kidding, right?" They both laughed.

"Did you suggest the name?"

"Yes, but it was one of the names she'd already picked out. Means all embracing. Sorry, gotta go."

Ahsha hung up and Haras sat back in the chair. She looked at the bed, and the fresh white sheets drew her like a comfort blanket.

When she awoke, Haras checked the address on the envelope of Gereg's returned letter, and called a taxi. She was keen to get out and see what she could discover. She picked up the long scarf she'd been advised to bring by the travel agent, and tied it loosely, throwing one end over her shoulder. A quick look in the mirror made her smile. She did look a bit like the locals she'd seen at the airport. Similar skin colour. If her eyes were closed, she'd probably be mistaken for one.

The taxi soon left the high-rise apartments behind and took her down narrow streets, some dusty, some cobbled and some sealed. Some were fresh and clean, some packed with people and every manner of thing. Haras held the seatbelt tightly, expecting the taxi to run someone over, or crash into other traffic, but it didn't.

In no time at all the taxi turned into a quiet cobbled street. The driver parked and pointed to a narrow alley, not wide enough for a car. The street name was neatly painted on the two-story corner building, standing out against the yellow painted plaster. Haras told the driver to wait until she knew if her grandparents were home or not. He nodded.

Haras wiped the sweat from her forehead. It wasn't that hot. She took a deep breath and scanned the row of plastered brick buildings, joined end to end along one side of the alley. Opposite the first door, painted bright blue, was a table and chair. It was set invitingly against a plastered brick wall that ran down the opposite side of the alley. It wasn't the door she was looking for. She glanced down at the terracotta pots and relaxed a little.

At the next door her excitement chased every hint of jet lag away. This was it. Her father and grandparents might still be here, right in front of her, right behind the wooden door. They might soon be sitting in those two black chairs, looking at the tree rambling over the alley wall, smelling the sweet spices ...

The wooden door was hard against her knuckles. She waited. She took her family photo from her wallet and her hands trembled. She held it tight, straining to make sense of voices inside. A man appeared and leaned on the door handle. Haras opened her mouth. He was unshaven and crumpled, as though he'd just woken up, completely out of place in this clean, quaint place. He studied Haras, but didn't smile or speak.

Haras stood there with her mouth open. He wasn't her father.

"I, I'm looking for my grandparents."

The man frowned. He almost spelling out the words. "You want?" He was obviously unfamiliar with English.

"Um, I ..." Haras showed him the photo. "I'm … my family."

The man called out something she didn't understand and a young boy came running to the door. The man pointed to the boy.

With a sinking heart, Haras realised her family must have moved on.

"What do you want?"

The boy spoke in recognizable English and Haras stopped trembling.

"I'm looking for my grandparents." She turned the photo so the boy could see it. "They lived here. Did they leave a forwarding address?" She held the photo up for the man to see as well. He took it, studied it for a while, turned it over, then gave it back. He spoke to the boy.

"Too long ago. Killed in a bomb blast … extremists."

Haras couldn't take it in.

"Killed?" Her legs felt weak. No, maybe he didn't understand. "They used to live here," she said.

"Yes, Dad does recognize them. They died. There was a bomb on the bus they were in."

Haras reached for the wall and steadied herself.

The man pulled the chair out for her and Haras flopped into it.

"Killed?" The words echoed in her head and her energy fled.

The man said something, before sitting down beside her. The boy ran inside and reappeared with a glass of water. With hunched shoulders, he held it out to Haras. She drank it without thinking.

"Were all three killed?" she asked as she held out the photo again.

"Three?" The boy spoke to his father.

"He doesn't know." The boy interpreted.

"An older couple. The newspaper said. They didn't rent this place long. Maybe a month. A man rented the place after them, but he didn't stay long either. He may have been their son. He was a foreigner."

The man scratched his stubble.

"Dad says he thought the man may have gone travelling … some place safer … far away? That's all he knows."

Haras's heart sank. *Far away* was where she'd just come from.

"You all right?" The taxi driver yelled out as he walked towards them.

Haras stood. She nodded and thanked the boy. She held out her hand to thank the man, and he suddenly smiled softly. He said something to his son and they both nodded. Haras stepped back. She couldn't look at the tenderness in his eyes.

"Dad says he's sorry."

"Thanks and thanks for the water," Haras said.

The cobblestones that seemed so smooth before, jutted up and she stumbling going back to the taxi. She rearranged her headscarf, throwing the end over her shoulder and pressed her eyes shut. She wasn't going to cry.

"Where to now?" The driver asked, looking through his rear view mirror.

Haras had wanted to visit the neighbours, but now she couldn't do that.

"The hostel. Back to the hostel, I mean hotel." The words stumbled out. They didn't even sound like her own. She wanted to be there, by herself, *right now*.

Back at the hotel Haras made a cup of coffee and sat for a moment in the communal kitchen. She let her heavy eyelids droop and then close. A young blonde-haired, blue-eyed couple came into the room. Newlyweds? They looked and sounded a bit Finnish, like Ollo. Haras was in no mood to talk, so she just nodded hello and headed for her room.

Again, Haras was glad she'd paid extra for a single room. She finished the coffee and took the urn from her backpack. As she traced the hieroglyphics with her finger, she thought of her mother's last words and her eyes brimmed over.

"Tell Deerg I'm sorry."

Throwing herself on the bed, she sobbed into the pillow, the first time in a long while. Were all her family destined to have short lives?

"Why did you all have to die? It's not fair!" She rolled over again and pummelled the pillow then sank into it. She let the sadness be swallowed by something stronger; a storm, a storm of pent-up angry emotions. When that abated, Haras rolled over again and lay staring at the ceiling, completely exhausted.

Some-time later she woke and for the second time, for want of anything better to do, made up her mind to stay. She couldn't think of anything else to do. There was nothing more important in her life, than finding her father. Her expanded horizons had shrunk again, but maybe if she stayed in the area … maybe she'd meet another Emme—someone who knew something that could help her. If bumping into Emme had been a sign, maybe there would be another one.

Haras blew her nose and noticed she was hungry. She washed her face and went down to reception.

The receptionist on duty looked up from his screen. His thick glasses made his dark eyes look enormous. He spoke excellent English, and was quite chatty, even though he kept checking his screen. Every so often, he flicked a wave of black hair away from his eyes and gave her his full attention. He told her about some eating-places and some other local places she might visit.

Haras began thinking he would keep her there all night with his talk, but another backpacker arrived at the door. Haras stepped away from the counter. The receptionist waved a pamphlet and Haras took it and escaped.

The eating-places were easy to find. Haras was glad to see the yellow M. She bought a burger meal and sat down outside the shop to enjoy it. She glanced at her watch - five p.m. There probably wasn't any Wi-Fi access around and even though she had a satellite phone, Ahsha would be at work, so she shouldn't really call her. She would try before she went to bed. What should she do next?

She opened the pamphlet and scanned it—tourist attractions. A map showed some ancient ruins but they weren't listed as a place to visit. The message on the urn came into her mind. *Find the ancient path*. Ancient ruins were bound to have ancient paths. She folded the pamphlet into her bag, finished her takeaway and headed back to the hotel.

The receptionist looked pleased at Haras's interest in the ruins. He told her it was on public land but it hadn't been developed for tourists. He pointed at her map. "The river used to be good for gold miners but I believe it dried up."

"Really?" Her mother's words popped into her mind. "Your father was besotted with the idea of gold digging."

Haras's mind began to race with possibilities. Had her father come looking for the ancient path? She leaned forward. "Are there any gold-miners still there?"

"Don't know sorry. I've never been out there." The receptionist glanced back at his screen, but Haras had more questions.

"Do you think I'd be able to explore the ruins?"

"Well, some people have been exploring out there. He took another pamphlet and opened it up. "Here." He pointed to a town near the ruins. "You could visit this town. Masam. They might be able to give you more information. I haven't heard of any recent explorers."

He gave her the details of a bus that would take her somewhere near Masam. There was only one bus a day. She would need a taxi from there to the town. He flicked his hair back again and folded the pamphlet.

"There's a couple of bed and breakfast places out there somewhere, otherwise go back into town." Haras read the name on his badge.

"Thanks, Ara."

Ara beamed a smile. "So, what are your plans for tonight?"

Haras regretted using his name. She wasn't flirting. She was being courteous. "It's been a long day. I need an early night." She turned. "Goodnight."

She felt his smile on her back as she walked away.

"Goodnight," he called after her.

Chapter 

Just in time. Haras grinned as she approached the counter the following morning. The couple she'd seen when she first arrived queued behind her. The receptionist was less likely to want to keep her talking when others were waiting. He was pushing his thick glasses back up his nose as he greeted her.

"Good morning! So, is it the ruins or shopping in the city today?"

His friendliness and curiosity didn't touch her.

"The ruins and shopping, but not in the city! I'll try Masam." Haras settled her account and made a quick exit.

Ancient ruins! Haras repeated the words in her mind, savouring them. The words themselves excited her and she couldn't wait to explore. It was a long shot, but maybe her father had been there digging for gold. She'd go there first and if she found nothing, she'd go back to her grandparents last address, and visit the neighbours. Although she'd need an interpreter with her if she went door knocking. She didn't relish the idea.

Haras found the bus stop and after a painfully long wait, was on her way. After an equally painful, long bus ride, she was waiting again, this time for a taxi.

As the taxi pulled up, Haras thought she saw Izzi drive past in a red sports car. She watched the car for a moment before getting into the taxi.

When Haras told the driver she wanted some camping gear and more information about the ruins, he said he knew just the shop.

It sounded good to Haras, and to her relief it wasn't long before she was standing outside a large general store in Masam. Klat's Store. The name was barely visible. It needed a fresh coat of paint.

As she opened the door, she decided it too would have needed a fresh coat of paint if it hadn't been glass. It was grimy, but the smell of baking and fresh coffee was welcoming.

Inside a few men were sitting around drinking coffee. They scrutinized her as though she was an alien. Their dark scowls made her feel nervous. Haras wished she'd worn her scarf and not her hat.

"Nellen! Nellen!" one of the men called out. The store owner? A female appeared wiping her hands on a red apron. Haras silently excused the poor woman for not cleaning the glass door. She looked like she was worked to the bone: there wasn't an ounce of fat on her. She took her apron off and gave Haras her full attention, after brushing back her grey hair. It didn't make her curls look any less scruffy. However, when she spoke, she spoke fluent English and was very helpful. Haras was taken aback. She wasn't expecting someone who looked as hard as a rock and worn out to be so pleasant.

Nellen showed Haras a map of the area, and chatted away about the ruins. There were two ways in. One by foot, the long way, would take about three days. She recommended that way. The other way was more dangerous because although it was shorter, you could easily get lost. The terrain was more difficult to climb, with lots of boulders, and if she went that way, she'd also need something like a 4WD to get as close as possible, or someone to drive her.

"Go the long way. You need enough food for a good three days in and three days out, plus however long you plan to be there. Although," she paused for a moment "… you might find some figs growing along the way, this time of year. That'll stretch your provisions. There's an old water fountain at the ruins, and I think there's a water pool somewhere near where the sealed road ends. How long do you think you'll stay at the ruins?"

"Maybe a day or two?"

"We could send someone in to check on you in four days' time and bring more food. That way you won't have to carry so much."

"Do you know someone?"

"Yes. He owns a bed and breakfast place not too far from here. Well, he used to run the place as one. I think he's retired from it now, or tries to be. Comes in here from time to time. Wife likes my chocolate cakes." She wiped her hands on her dress. "In fact he's coming in later today for some. Wife's birthday, I think."

Haras took out her wallet. "Maybe I could get a ride out there with him?"

"Too late in the day, I'd say. Half a day's driving if you take the long way, then a couple of hour's walk, maybe more. It'd be dark before he got to the ruins and with his wife's birthday … I don't know. You are probably better off walking the other way. Get a ride back. That way you can do your exploring."

"Would gold prospectors have gone there?"

"Gold-seekers. Some did, tried their hand at panning in the stream that used to run near the ruins."

"Any prospectors still out there?"

"Don't think so. They dried up along with the stream after the big earthquake. It took part of the road out. That's why it's so difficult to get there. We still carry a bit of equipment for the occasional explorer, like you, though."

A brawny man looked up, over a pair of dusty glasses and scowled. "No-one has been down to the ruins looking for gold for years." He spat the words in Haras's direction. "No big earthquakes since then, either." He sounded as hard as granite, and his English, startled Haras. Others joined in. She couldn't pick out any English words, but their manner was menacing. She didn't like to ask what it was they were so heated about.

"No gold-seekers, but as I said, sometimes we get someone interested in exploring the ruins, and the council checks the place from time to time, making sure it's safe," Nellen said.

Her comment brought another burst of angry sounds and heated conversation among the men that disturbed Haras.

Despite the warnings and discouraging comments from some of the men - or maybe because of them, Haras dug her heels in and decided she was going to see the ruins anyway. She wasn't going to let their words make a wall to stop her. Maybe she would find the ancient path of her urn among them. Maybe her father had gone that way or someone was there who knew where he'd gone.

Haras bought the map, a lightweight tent, and a sleeping bag. She took Nellen's advice and bought enough dry food for the three days it would take to get there and three fresh filled rolls.

"You need to let me know the day before, so I have enough time to get someone to go out there and pick you up, or drop off some food." She estimated a price for the service and Haras agreed to pay on delivery. They exchanged phone numbers and Haras thanked her.

She was about to open the store door when a young man entering the shop, did it for her. She looked up into a shock of curly black hair. She forgot to say thank you, as she looked at his bronzed face. His brown eyes shone through long, dark lashes. For an instance, Haras wanted to lose herself in their softness. She lowered her eyes and remembered her manners. "Thank you!"

"My pleasure!"

She caught a whiff of his aftershave as she passed. It had the same effect on her as a bunch of perfumed roses, but she didn't dare stop and inhale it or comment on how nice it was.

He didn't close the door after her. For a moment, she felt his eyes on her back. She didn't look back but nearly bumped into someone; a woman, bent over, aged like a crooked grey stick.

The woman scowled at her and shook her head and her finger. "No! Bad ruins! You no go." Her gaping yellow teeth and her warning gave Haras a fright but didn't deter her.

How did *she* know she was going to the ruins? Maybe she'd overheard them talking, or was it her new camping gear?

Haras walked on, dismissing the old woman's words. She was thinking about dark curly hair and sparkling eyes. What a contrast his attitude was to the scowling men and the *ancient* woman.

Haras pulled her hat down hard. She was here on a mission and the only man she was looking for was her father!

Father? Her hand flew to her open mouth. She'd forgotten to show the photo.

Haras raced back to the store. She ignored the cold reception as she looked around. The curly-haired man wasn't there. She was disappointed. She passed the photo around and asked if anyone recognised the people in the photo. They were all strangely vague. It was a long time ago. They might have.

Haras clothed her arms around her body as if that could shift the sudden coldness. She didn't stay long.

Chapter K

Knitting her brows, Haras grumbled. She wasn't used to carrying such a lot of gear. Travelling on foot wasn't as easy as she'd imagined. Sticky drips trickled under her hat and her boots began to feel like rocks, weighing her down. They scraped and crunched against small stones and the noise began to irritate her. She wished she'd gone the other way, the shorter walk, the way most people went. She wished she'd paid for a taxi, or waited a day or so and hired someone to drive her. She wished she didn't feel so darn harassed, like her name, again.

Haras remembered the times she'd leaned back against her gran for a hug, and right then she felt like she needed that hug. This place wasn't her home. Why hadn't she thought this through? She was in a strange country. She didn't know anyone here. What if she couldn't make it to the ruins? She wished there was someone to give her a reassuring hug. A father's hug, that's what she needed.

Just when she had talked herself into going back, she came to the end of the road.

"Find the ancient path?" Haras frowned. How could she? She'd been walking for hours. Her map only showed the modern roads and she'd come to the end of the road that went anywhere near anything like the pyramid-shaped ruins. Haras wished she had her 'Too Hard' basket with her. If she had, she would've thrown the urn and her back pack into it, her boots too! First her boots. She was definitively not cut out for what this journey was hinting at becoming.

Before sitting down, Haras pulled out her drinking bottle and sucked on it strongly. She'd stuffed the urn with nuts and took that out too. She placed it on the ground beside her and took a small handful of nuts before squinting at the distant ruin. The sky was growing black, tossing up menacing clouds. The wind caught at her map.

What a shame the map isn't more useful. She folded it and reached for the urn, but knocked it over.

"Oh rats!" Ahsha's favourite expletive popped from her mouth, as the urn rolled over the cliff. She heard the metallic sound as it hit the rocks below.

"Terrific!" She pictured the urn dented or lost. The thought triggered a snake of anger that rose up and swallowed her tiredness.

Judging how close she could get to the cliff edge was tricky. Haras squatted down and got up a few times before she felt safe enough to prostrate herself. She inched her way forward and nervously peered over the edge. There was a rocky ledge below, but she couldn't see the urn. She inched a bit further and saw a cave.

A place to camp if it rains. She estimated the distances. If she lowered herself onto the ledge underneath, she might be able to check out the cave. The urn probably rolled into it.

With all her camping gear in place, she stretched out on the rock, pressing her stomach down into the ground. It wasn't much of a hold, but she inched her way backwards until her legs were hanging over the side of the rock. She could almost reach the ledge underneath.

So far so good!

She grabbed at some weeds as the weight of her body took her right over the edge. She landed hard against her backpack, arms flailing and lay trembling with the shock, but not for long. She dusted herself off, picked up her hat and bent to go into the cave. A trail of nuts directed her to the urn and lid. It only had a small dent, but as she picked the lid up, something rattled inside. She turned the lid over and tried to twist it open, but the base was firmly attached. She would need pliers to peel the sides of the top up to see what was rattling inside.

Haras scooped up some of the nuts and put them back in, thinking she might need them, even if they were dusty.

As she reached down for the last of the nuts, she thought she saw something move behind her. Iciness grasped at her and she jumped sideways. Were there snakes in the rocks? Her eyes raced over the ground, over every rock. *Nothing!* Her hands fell to her sides.

Need to be more careful. Make some noise to frighten them off.

She packed the urn away and scrutinized the area. There was a steep but clear track hugging the rock edge. The possibility of ancient paths fuelled her steps. She walked on until she spotted an old tree branch wedged between two rocks. It would make a good walking stick. She paused before climbing over the rocks to take a closer look. It certainly was old and gnarly, but it wasn't just a branch. Someone had carved a handle on one end. Just what she needed - a walking stick to frighten off the snakes. No-one had told her to be wary of snakes, but what if there were some?

The stick was wedged in tightly, but Haras worked it back and forth and wriggled it out. She tested its strength by striking it against a rock. It reminded her of a film Ahsha had invited her to see. She'd told Ahsha she wasn't interested. It sounded too religious for her. Ahsha had gone without her but insisted on telling her the story afterwards - something about a man who struck a rock and water had gushed out for him.

"Yes!" It was still a strong walking stick and suitably loud, but *no*, it didn't cause a stream to flow.

What an odd thought.

Haras didn't expected water to gush out. She had her water bottle and had been told there was a pool of water somewhere nearby. She pounded the stick loudly on the ground as she marched on.

She furrowed her brows and a hiss of annoyance escaped from her mouth.

It wasn't the easiest of tracks to follow. Sometimes she had to climb over quite large and jagged boulders. They looked like they'd fallen down from above. Eventually she came out into a wide flat area. It reminded her of an oasis in the desert. It was such a peaceful place with wild flowers and soft grass, the perfect place to pitch her tent.

Haras plucked a flower and held it near her nose. The smell was refreshing, enhanced by the low bubble of water nearby. She looked around, but couldn't see any water. She took her backpack off and ran her fingers along the stem of a wild millet plant, gleaning the seeds; glad she'd studied edible weeds. In the shade of a rock she spotted a Hawksbeard weed and picked a few leaves, savouring the carrot flavour. She was tempted to take off her boots but didn't. Instead, she sat down and suddenly believed the stories about flowers making people fall asleep.

Chapter

Lethargic feelings leapt away with the sound of falling stones. Was something or someone behind her? Haras listened intently. Were there boots crunching the stones along the cliff edge? She leaned forward, but large grey boulders blocked her view. She licked her dry lips, then grabbed her gear and rushed through the grass towards the sound. She placed her free hand on the cold stone that jutted out from the cliff edge and listened, but her chest thumped so loudly it obscured any other sounds.

She leaned round for a better view. A breath of wind ruffled through the grass, exposing flat stones here and there. Two butterflies danced upwards from a group of wild pink flowers, jerking her eyes away from the cliff wall. Out of the corner of her eye, she saw a dark treelike shape. A statue?

No, it wasn't a statue. It was a man, an old man, tall and straight. He was standing on a rock looking into the distance. Haras titled her head.

There was an air of peace and serenity about him that made him look as if he'd been standing there for a long time. Haras followed his gaze to some jagged mossy rocks to the left of the cliff. What was he looking at? Should she go back or not? Too late. He turned and saw her.

"Ah, I see you found my old walking stick." He waved what she supposed was his new one in her direction. It didn't look that new.

There was something familiar about him, something that reminded her of Emme. It wasn't just the colour of his hair. She approached him cautiously.

A gold-seeker?

He took his sunglasses off and Haras thought his eyes twinkled below his scruffy white brows.

"I found it wedged—"

"Finders keepers," he said.

He put his glasses back on. "You may need it. What are you doing on my goat path?"

"Your goat path?" Heat pumped into her face. She had been told it was a public place! She opened her mouth to argue her defence, but something authoritative in his demeanour made her back down.

His words reminded her of the "The Three Billy Goats Gruff" fairy story. He didn't look anything like what she imagined a goat-herd looked like though, except for his wool jacket. It was nearing the end of its life, but his shoes were new and his trousers looked that way as well.

"Yes, once upon a time, I used this track to lead my goats and a few gold-seekers to water."

There was a glow of light on his high cheek bones, almost angelic and his chuckle came from his eyes as well as his mouth.

So he wasn't a gold-seeker. He was a goat-herd!

The man interrupted her thoughts by extending his arm towards her. Beneath his frayed coat sleeve, was an equally weathered hand holding a crumpled business card.

"I was told you were heading this way. A friend saw you at Klat's. I wanted to make sure you found the safest path."

"My name's Renner," he said with a smile.

"Oh, you're the bed and breakfast man." Haras said reading the words on the card.

"What? Did they mention us at Klat's store?

"Yes." Haras nodded.

"We used to do bed and breakfast, hence the business card. Why? Do you need somewhere to stay?"

"I might, but aren't you the person Klat's store said they would organise to pick me up from the ruins or deliver food?"

"I haven't heard anything about that yet. Left my phone in the car."

"The shop assistant said she would arrange for someone to meet me at the ruins - bring in some food or provide transport out."

"Okay. Sometimes on my way to Klat's I do a detour. This place is an oasis of peace ... Anyway, just follow the path beyond the cleft, as I said, and take the right. No need to be anxious on the right path." He smiled at his pun and it dabbed at her anxiety.

"Call me if you have any trouble. I presume you have a satellite phone - no mobile reception out here."

"Yep. I hope I won't need it, but thanks for your help." She was surprised a stranger would care enough to help her find a safe way to the ruins. Did he have ulterior motives? Haras decided not. He was a lot different from the other locals, who spat scowling looks at her.

"The water sounds very close doesn't it?" He pointed beyond her vision with his walking stick.

The low rumble was just audible. It didn't sound as close as it did beyond the boulder. Haras tried to see what he was pointing at, presumably the water, but she couldn't see anything.

"It is close, but you can't go straight to it," he said. "It's also very hard to find. If you stand on this stone, you may catch a glimpse of it."

She stood on the rock he had vacated. A drift of mist lifted as a gust of wind swirled down from above the rocks. "The clouds look a lot closer from up here."

A glint of light caught her attention. "I see the water. It looks as black as the sky over there."

"Up close, it's the cleanest water I've ever seen." Renner pointed towards what he called a cleft in one of the rocks and suggested she head in that direction. She would easily make it before the rain.

"Cleft?" She squinted towards where he was pointing. She hadn't heard that word since - when - since her gran's funeral? Yes. She remembered asking her mother what the word meant – *He hideth my soul in the cleft of the rock.*

Haras saw the crack in the rock. Had an earthquake created the crevice?

"You'll find a path beyond the cleft. Follow it and take the right where it divides. Even though the left looks more promising, its promises are empty." He scratched his chin and looked away. Haras tilted her head to catch what he was saying.

"It isn't a short cut. Loose rocks! Slippery in the evening mist." He turned to look at her as she listened intently. "The right path is a hidden gem … I knew you would need someone or something to point it out."

"Doesn't the left path have a danger sign?" Haras asked and then felt foolish. He'd said it was his path, not a public place.

"It did have, but someone kept moving it. Maybe they thought they could benefit from people suffering a lot of hard knocks."

"It did?" Haras thanked him. She was anxious about the path. She would believe his words when she'd travelled the path.

"Many have travelled this way before, although few found what they were seeking. Oh, and you'll find a suitable place to camp near the pool." With this, his manner changed and his frown caught Haras off guard.

Looking at the sky, Renner repeated his advice. "Remember, the right path is the right one."

Haras titled her head. "Ha!"

Without another word, Renner strode out in the opposite direction, looking too fit for a man with such white hair. White hair that was rather long for someone his vintage. He waved her on, but Haras continued watching him. Half expecting him to run.

Each step disturbed flowers peppered throughout the long grass, causing a few butterflies to flicker out beside him. She hoped she would be as sprightly as he was when she was his age.

He turned and smiled before disappearing, and his smile leapt inside her. She was glad he wasn't telling her to get off his land. Would she have listened to him if he had? No. She would've waited until he left, and then continued. There was a storm brewing and she didn't want to go the long way round.

She turned Renner's card over in her hand and read it before pocketing it.

Chapter 

Misgivings gone, Haras stepped down from the rock. The cleft disappeared from view again. She trusted Renner's advice, but the long grass looked a good place for snakes. She set off in the direction of the opening, waving the walking stick like a minesweeper through the grass in front of her.

She came to the edge of the grassy slope relieved that she hadn't encountered any snakes. The rock towered up before her again. She clambered over some boulders and saw the entrance: the cleft. But finding a way in wasn't easy as fallen rocks obscured the entrance.

Seeing some ripe figs, she reached through a sprawling blackberry vine to pick some. The vine scratched through her long sleeved top, and she jerked upright. The dent in the urn flashed into her mind. She gritted her teeth and fumed until she realized what she was doing. Irritability signalled tiredness and hunger. She savoured a few ripe figs to deal with the hunger. Dealing with tiredness would have to wait.

There were a few more boulders to climb before she could stand in the cleft, but finally she was there.

The coolness of the crevice surprised her. She placed her hands flat on the rock wall to soak up the cold. It felt so smooth and solid. She closed her eyes and pressed her hot check against it too.

The sides of the rock towered up over her. They touched at the top forming a roof. She wasn't sure if she should stay or go on. How long would it take to get to the pool? She could see the promised path. Renner was right about that. Haras decided against staying and pressed forward.

As she picked her way among the stones, she was struck by how different it was to the grassy oasis on the other side of the cleft.

The path didn't get any easier as she descended. She stopped and removed her hat. Should she return to the cleft of the rock and try the path in the morning? It *was* getting dark. She pressed on.

Something wobbled beneath her feet. It was long and black. She leapt backwards, then turned and ran.

Stopping at a safe distance, Haras looked back. The long black thing was still there. She watched it. *A tree root?* Her heart stopped racing as she retraced her steps.

She poked it with her walking stick. *Only a tree, root but where's the tree it belongs to?* All she saw was a shadow in the misty distance. How black the clouds looked. That settled it. She was going back to the cleft.

Another root grabbed at her feet but she didn't stop. Just as she reached the cleft, the clouds fulfilled their promise. Large raindrops pelted down around her. *That was close.*

Chest heaving, she shook the drops from her hat and sat down on a large flat boulder, perfectly placed for a chair. She looked up. Water trickled down the sides of the rock.

Haras was glad for a dry base. She found a curved branch and used it to sweep an area clear of the small stones that covered the ground. It took quite a while to make a flat area big enough to sleep on. She opened the tent and used it as a ground cover under her sleeping bag.

The night closed in quickly. Haras checked the time on her phone and calculated the time difference. It was still too early to phone Ahsha. Her lunch break wasn't for another hour. Haras turned her phone light on, devoured the last filled roll and took out a few nuts. She cleaned them one at a time by rolling them over and over in her t-shirt.

Thunder hammered away in the distance, but Haras turned her phone light off. She lay down and pulled the sleeping bag up. It worked like a comfort blanket, making her feel safer. *He hideth my soul in the cleft of the rock.* The words repeated in her mind but as hard as she tried, she couldn't remember the rest of the song. Why did anyone need to hide their soul?

Haras had planned to stay awake to call Ahsha, but began to doze. An image flashed into her mind, an image of her gran in her coffin. She sat up again and fumbled quickly for her phone. It's light revealed a few wet patches bleeding down the rock, even though the rain had stopped and the ground was dry.

She checked her watch. *Perfect!* She didn't feel safe with sadness tonight. Ahsha would be on her lunch break.

Haras picked her way over the stones towards the entrance of the cleft, hoping for satellite reception. She couldn't help sucking in her breath as her soft bare feet made contact with the stones.

Ahsha must have been waiting for her call. She answered immediately.

"So, how's it going?"

"Great. I'm sheltering in the *cleft of the rock*!"

"What, in Christ?" Haras enjoyed the excitement in Ahsha's voice.

"Well if he's here, I can't see him. No, a real cleft in a real rock!" Haras laughed as she explained where she was and how Renner's words had reminded her of the song at her gran's funeral.

"Well Christ is real too —"

Haras ignored Ahsha's comment. "… and I nearly bumped into a real cool guy! He opened the door for me at the store where I bought a few camping things."

Ahsha laughed. "So, it's not just a pilgrimage, searching for your father?"

"You know the only man I'm looking for is my father, but—his eyes …"

"You're definitely ready for a date Haras." They both laughed.

"Do you think you'll find your father in the ruins?"

"Not very likely, but he did have gold fever, and someone said they didn't know if anyone was still out here. Anyway, ancient ruins sound mysterious and exciting. There might be an ancient path here, maybe even the one mentioned on my urn."

Ahsha's response sounded dubious and her doubt was catching. Haras rubbed the back of her neck. The muscles were tight from carrying her gear. They changed the subject and talked until Ahsha had to go back to work.

"Sleep safe."

"Thanks, Ahsha. Enjoy your day."

Haras made it carefully back to her sleeping bag and dusted her feet on the outside.

Something brushed against her hair. Haras swiped wildly. Every hint of happiness and sleepiness fled. Her heart thumped in her ears.

Shadows flickered in eerie spots in the phone light. Haras held her breath and stared hard. Cold air flapped past her face. She shone the light up and caught a glimpse of wings. A bat! A tiny bat. Her shoulders sagged. At least she hadn't made her bed in a large colony of them, and with bats around, there shouldn't be too many insects.

She berated herself for being so jumpy. She grabbed her makeshift pillow and fluffed it up before relaxing back into her sleeping bag.

Chapter 14

Sun and sleep washed all Haras's negative thoughts away. She stood in the morning sunlight and drank in the clean, almost floral air, yet rocks replaced the proliferation of flowers she'd seen on the other side of the cleft. Some still shone from the previous night's washing. The stony path surprised her. It wasn't slippery. The sun had already dried it out, and even the scratches on her arms weren't bothering her.

"This is the life!" She half expected her words to echo back. They didn't.

She was glad she'd breakfasted on the figs and blackberries at the entrance to the cleft. It didn't look like there would be any more fruit trees down this side of the mountain, and their juice meant she didn't need to drink as much water.

Shoulders back, she strode out, slowing only when she saw the tree root she'd tripped on the day before. It belonged to a gnarly old fig tree. She could see it clearly now, greyed by the weather, blending into the rocks around it. Rock and tree were both still and lifeless.

She continued at a slower pace, to take in the scenery. Butterflies flickered above the few patches of grass. They reminded her of Renner striding across the oasis. She remembered his advice about a good camping spot. It was probably good advice.

Haras was glad the path was still visible. She saw evidence of animal grazing here and there and was glad they'd left some blackberries for her to graze on too.

By mid-afternoon, a few clouds had gathered and for a while, she upped her leisurely pace. A particularly juicy crop of berries caught her attention.

As she reached in to pick them she noticed a rusty old "danger" sign half buried in the ground. *Must be the one Renner spoke of.*

She looked around for another path. She couldn't see any. The one she was on narrowed ahead, because of the sprawling blackberries. She heard a low rumble deep down, with bubbles dancing above. The sound came from her left not the right. *No wonder people tended to go left.*

The path soon divided just as Renner had said, and she took the right, giving herself a tick for following advice.

It wasn't long before the ground changed to stone and boulders and then she saw it, the pool of water! It was stunning, clear blue glass, like a mirror framed in rocks, not black as she remembered glimpsing it with Renner—not rumbling. It drew her like a magnet. She ached to be engulfed in its freshness, to let the dust and weariness wash away.

She clambered over rocks to the edge. The water looked deep and clean. It reflected a small patch of blue in the cloudy sky. She dropped her backpack and squatted on the rock. She could see the rocky riverbed beneath as she trailed her hands through the water. A few clouds darkened the water and she looked up. She needed to pitch her tent before it rained. An overhanging rock looked like it would offer shelter. Haras picked up her pack and pitched her tent there.

The cloud passed by without bringing the rain it promised, so Haras untied her boots and wriggled her toes in the sand. The water was so clear, and she was so sticky. She couldn't resist a quick swim.

She rummaged for her travel towel and was soon standing at the water's edge in her black sports bra and shorts. One toe went in, then another. Shoulders hunched up, hands bunched against her collarbones, she took a few steps.

Waist deep, arms in the air she held her breath, then slipped under. *Not so bad!*

On her knees, face in the water, she opened her eyes to pristine pebbles, mostly white. She walked on her hands then took a deep breath and pushed off, floating out. The pumping of her heart was louder than the ripples she made.

The rocks soon fell away and she couldn't see the bottom. She opened her eyes wider, trying to penetrate the darkness. A shadowy movement attacked her calm.

Even as Haras began crashing back through the water, she told herself not to be silly. Yet this self-talk didn't stop her until she saw the rocks beneath. She stood up trembling and wiped the water from her eyes. There wasn't anything but clear clean water. She chided herself again for being so cowardly.

Feeling calmer, she sank back down into the water and rolled over onto her back.

He leads me over reposing waters. The words popped into her mind. Where had she heard them before? At her gran's funeral? *No.* She'd seen them on one of the sympathy cards she'd found among her mother's things. She'd read it then thrown it out as she didn't know the sender.

Haras rolled over again and stood up. Her fingers were stained from the blackberries and she rubbed them, but the colour remained. Her stomach growled. She scanned the dry rocky areas for Abal plants and spotted some stiff green branches in a sandy spot among the rocks. She swam closer to identify the plant. *Yes.* She could see the distinctive red antlers. It was an Abal plant.

The rocks warmed her feet. She formed her hair into a small ponytail and squeezed it, as she dripped her way over the rocks. The sand stuck between her toes as she enjoyed the small sugar fix from the flowers.

That evening as she sat looking at the sky, a few stars began to twinkle in the blackness. Haras couldn't resist singing.

"Twinkle, Twinkle Little Star, how I …" She didn't finish. If she could see the stars it meant no rain! She stretched upwards and called out, "Yes, keep twinkling!"

She sat stargazing for some time thinking about distant worlds. What was beyond, beyond? Before long, a wave of tiredness reminded her of the time. She rubbed her eyes. Ahsha would be on her lunch break in an hour. She texted her a message, *tired but safe.*

With the flaps of her little tent tightly closed, she told herself she *was* safe. Nothing *was* lurking in the night.

"I'm not afraid," she said aloud to bolster her confidence. Her words echoed back in her mind as she drifted off to sleep.

Chapter 15

Every muscle tensed and Haras sat bolt upright. She sat listening, wide awake. A solitary bird was marking its territory with sound. Haras slumped back. She'd been dreaming! It was morning and she'd slept right through the night.

She kicked the sleeping bag off and opened the tent flap. The beauty of the clean pool water swept through her mind and she found her way to it. Her clothes fell onto the rock where she dropped them and the water grabbed at her ankles, then her legs. It was cold until she allowed it to wrap her in its freshness. She rolled onto her back and could have floated on the water forever, but breakfast and the ruins beckoned her.

She climbed back over the rocks and found herself looking at a rusty old watering can. She picked it up and ran her thumb along the side. *Not quite Aladdin's lamp.*

She hadn't seen anything like it before. Its antique look beguiled her, and even though one side was partly rusted through, she took it back to the tent. Perhaps others had done the same thing, each taking it a little further.

Haras held it up for another inspection, and decided it would look great in a xeric garden, a garden that didn't need a watering can. She packed up her tent and tied the can to her pack.

It wasn't long before she was clambering over the rocks that edged the pool, heading for the ravine. She tied her boots to her backpack and waded through small pools of water. Occasionally she stopped to inspect a pool, hoping the ones ahead were not too deep. She didn't want to have to swim.

Finally, she stood on a rock near the ravine entrance. A small bush grew right out of the rock and she studied it as she put her boots back on. It always intrigued her how plants could take root in the most rugged places, producing enough pressure to force rocks apart and even crack them.

As she came through the large gate-like rocks, sunrays suddenly burst out through the cloud. She gasped in awe as the words Ahsha had written on the farewell card jumped into her mind. *"God makes the gate of morning and dusk shout for joy."*

The sun beamed and she did too. The gate of the morning was shouting for joy and she felt like laughing.

A blessing? Ahsha always used such old-fashioned words, yet here it was somehow appropriate.

She stopped and listened. The silence was palpable. She waited. A bird flew past and Haras fumbled for her phone. She took a photo and texted Ahsha: *Gates of blessing shouting for joy.* She knew Ahsha would appreciate that, and maybe it would stop her worrying.

Haras didn't feel as sure-footed as she continued picking her way among the rocks. Slipping on a sharp stone made her wonder if she would be *shouting* for a doctor.

Another world opened before her, and it wasn't an oasis. Haras resisted an odd desire to water the ground. It was rusty like the watering can, a stony bed where she presumed the water had once flowed. It meandered in the direction of the ruins, which she could now see. She concluded it must've been the spring Nellen had mentioned, and she made it her path.

As she walked, she came upon tell-tale signs that proved her right: an old pan, a bent spoon, a pick head, and bits of glass from old bottles, even a rusted-out frying pan. She fought the urge to collect more rusty things. She liked the look of them. They would all look great in a xeric garden too, or in a painting. She satisfied her collecting urge by taking a few photos.

The edge of a partially buried gold pan, almost tripped her. She crouched down and pulled at it. It was stuck hard. She worked it back and forwards.

Finally, it loosened its grip on the stony ground. A flat stone lay nearby and she used it to scrape some of the hard clay away. Brushing her finger over the rust, she couldn't tell if the markings were just the effect of the rust or if there were words inscribed on it. It needed washing. She kept holding it. Maybe she would try some panning.

All manner of questions came into her mind about the life of a gold prospector. What did they eat? Where did they get their food from? Did they crave solitude? She continued eyes on the ground, in case there were any large gold nuggets.

What do you really treasure? The thought interrupted her imaginings.

What do I treasure? She'd never really thought about it. She loved the bracelet Ahsha had given her, but if she lost it, it was replaceable. Ahsha was so different from her, yet she was a kind of treasure. But not a treasure Haras would stay home for.

A boyfriend? She didn't have a boyfriend. She had once had a relationship she thought was going somewhere, but it didn't last much past her mother's death. He wanted fun and didn't know how to deal with her grief.

Haras knew she would have treasured her father, if she had known him, but then Ahsha was the only teenager she knew who put a high value on hers. The way Ahsha talked about both her parents, even though they were divorced, was a lot nicer than any other teenager she knew.

Haras decided her real father would be a treasure. Again, as she usually did when she thought about him, she wished she'd known him. She built an image of him as one she could treasure. Her image wasn't like the one her mother had painted, but Haras knew broken relationships often left people like a broken pot. Sometimes she felt like one. Sometimes she let sadness coil around her chest.

Chapter 16

Exclamatory noises from the direction of the ruins startled Haras. Was someone there? She strained to hear, but the noises stopped. Haras did too and licked her lips. She increased her pace.

The top of the ruins peeked above some rocks. They weren't far away, but the stony bed was disappearing among the undergrowth. Purple flowers were snatching at her path as well.

In the early afternoon, a few goats near the base of the ancient ruins caught Haras's attention. Perhaps there was a goat-herd in the vicinity. That would account for the voice … or was it goats she'd heard?

Haras pulled her hat off and held it with her chin to free her hands. She gathered the bottom of her hair into one hand and ran her other hand up the back of her damp neck a few times. She was thirsty. She replaced her hat and sat down. One or two small mouthfuls of water was all she could afford. She let the first mouthful slowly trickle down her throat, then checked her watch. She was glad she'd woken at sunrise. She'd made excellent time, better time than the 'good three days' the shop assistant at Klat's had thought it would take.

Haras spluttered, water going down the wrong way as she remembered some of the jokes the men in the store had made.

Because no-one has been there for some years!

Well she was here now! Everything looked so peaceful. Had the locals deliberately tried to scare her off, or was there some other history she was yet to discover? She dismissed the uneasy feeling she got when she looked at the ruins. She had insisted on going despite the warnings and now, here she was and everything looked as it should. Actually, it looked even better.

Among a group of trees was one that looked like a fig. She hoped it was. Figs would satisfy her thirst and meant water was nearby. The grass was quite luxuriant, so Haras headed towards the trees. As she neared the trees, the ground muddied her boots. Annoyed, she looked for dry ground to the rocks beyond. She stepped onto a decaying branch and immediately regretted it. The branch sank beneath her. Haras wobbled and leap backwards just in time. *Phew! That was close!*

She poked the ground to see how deep the mud was. The walking stick went down about half a metre. Deep enough for her to get stuck. She poked at the mud to find a way to firmer ground and made her way to the tree. It was a fig tree! It still had plenty of figs too, so Haras feasted again. As far as she could see, it was the only fig tree.

It didn't take her long to find the old fountain. Someone had carved a cross into the rock. Haras took her hat off and fanned her face before taking a photo. She knew Ahsha would appreciate the Christian symbolism. She sent the photo to her with the text *Water from the rock!*

It looked as though there had been a water pipe at some time, but it was almost completely rusted away. She was delighted to see the water still trickling down. It had stained the stone but looked clean. A few purple poppy-like flowers had sprouted up near the base, which led Haras to conclude that the water was constant in its flow.

It took a while to fill her bottle but she didn't mind. Having water meant she had time. She wouldn't need to go back to the pool. She satisfied her thirst then scooped water up from the foot of the rock to wash the gold pan. Something slithered across her foot. It was so fast it startled her and she leaped back fearing the worst.

Do you have to jump at every little thing?

She poked around with her walking stick, knowing her reprimand wouldn't help.

Probably a lizard. Whatever it was, it was gone. She turned back to the pan and continued cleaning it.

An image of a cross had been scratched into the metal, similar to the image on the rocks. Haras frowned. It seemed a weird coincidence to discover one in front of her and another in the pan she was holding.

She didn't spend much time wondering. Instead, she washed her hands, filled her bottle again, and started towards the ruins … and there they were. Her mouth flew open. Areas of smooth, shiny marble-like granite, contrasted with rough areas of rock. She immediately loved the look of the different strata colour and texture. Some matched the carpet of small purple flowers around the base. At the top, the rock had been eroded leaving pointed cone shapes, crowning what looked like a cave. *A good place to camp … protection from rain!*

Haras noted the blue sky, but also remembered how quickly the clouds had come from nowhere. They didn't always bring rain though. Not like the ones she knew at home … well, what used to be home. Predicting the weather was much easier there.

Thoughts of home triggered a muddle of gloom. Again, she wished her mother was there to talk to. She really did love her mother. If only she'd told her so before she passed, but she'd been too busy trying to hear what her mother was trying to say. Her tongue had been clamped to the roof of her mouth.

Haras removed her hat and wiped the wetness from her eyes. She put it back on and began climbing up the slope. As she did, loose stones went spilling down behind her and she felt herself slipping with them. She steadied herself and stood for a moment gazing out across the land.

Chapter 17

Keeping her eyes glued to the ground, and her hand glued to her walking-stick, helped Haras not to slip, but it didn't help her to see where she was going. She almost missed a rock sprouting up in a mushroom shape. It looked like a plinth, just right for exhibiting the gold pan. She placed the pan on the rock and took a step back to admire it. *Perfect!* Something unusual for her photo collection. She left it there.

Up ahead, the ground looked surer. As she picked her way around some larger rocks, she hoped it was.

Climbing was easier without the pan. It wasn't long before she found what looked like the entrance she'd seen from below. She ran her hand over a small section of the arch-like opening. It was smooth, as if many hands had done the same thing. A few shafts of light gave the inside a cathedral-like appearance but there was no plaster or segments of plaster on the walls. There was nothing that indicated it had been anything like a cathedral. Most of the interior rooms, if they had been carved out, were now blocked by large boulders. She couldn't tell how far back they might have gone, if at all. She was disappointed. Why were they called *ancient* ruins? She saw no indication of what she'd call *ancient* workmanship, no carved stones. The large cracked stone steps didn't look ancient to her either.

The first set of steps took her up one level. She squeezed past what she imagined was caved-in roof rubble and saw an old wooden plank. It made a good seat and Haras stopped. A set of boot prints were facing her. Someone else must've thought the same thing.

She sat and placed her own boots in the indents. They were bigger than hers were. How long had the prints been there? She scraped the sand with her stick and something round caught her eye.

It was a metal button, perhaps it was Victorian. Haras smiled and pocketed the button. She didn't think it was valuable except as historical evidence. It could mean gold prospectors had been in the area. Maybe the boot-prints belonged to one of them. The marks may have been there for years. Haras patted her pocket. It was her little treasure and it cheered her up.

Continuing up the steps, she found the cave she'd seen from the ground. There were more boot-prints.

With water bottle in hand, she gazed out across the purple flowered landscape. *What a great view!*

She leaned over the rock and smiled. An image of Rapunzel using her hair as a ladder crossed her mind, and she smoothed her own *princess* hair. Shoulders back she imagined the ruins as her tower. She made a careful search of the landscape, nose still in the air and decided she was Lady of her own journey. Whoever belonged to the prints was long gone. She couldn't see anyone for miles.

The air was full of the smell of fragrant flowers. The sky was still blue and she had arrived safely. An ancient path was still a possibility.

But what if you can't find the path?

The question darted in, bringing melancholy with it. Her strength ebbed away and she felt her small, real, harassed self again. Had she come to a dead end?

Haras felt in her pocket for the button and looked at it more closely. She put it in her moneybag, which seemed a safest place.

The night came on quickly and was unusually still and warmer than the previous nights. Haras lay on top of her sleeping bag, chewing the remains of her dry evening meal. She went over the plans she'd made for the following day. She would take a closer look around the ruins. Maybe there were signs of an ancient path. Maybe she would find where it led and solve the mystery of her urn. Maybe …

Haras drifted off to sleep but woke suddenly, anxious and sweating. She tried to reassure herself. It was only a dream, but the dream was so vivid. There had been a goat-herd with yellowing teeth like the *ancient* woman she'd seen outside Klat's store. He had pointed his stick towards a dark muddy river. "Don't enter that path," he'd warned. He held a gold pan in his other hand and spoke more softly so she had to lean closer to hear.

"Avoid it! Turn away from it." He laboured the point before turning the pan over. She saw the fountain cross scratched into the pan, only it looked as though there was a diamond where the water came out.

It was still very dark, but the dream felt so real, Haras wondered what it could mean, if anything. Panning for gold had crossed her mind a few times. The warning sounded like her mother's angry voice. She had warned her, many times about the lure of gold. Now it sounded in her dreams! Haras didn't want to step in the mud again so she wasn't planning to go down that path. Maybe she would start looking for the ancient path by the cross … the water fountain … Haras dozed off again.

Chapter 18

Early bird! Did it get the worm? Haras rubbed her eyes and searched the dawn sky, but couldn't see where the shrill song came from. She shook the dust from her bedding, and folded it away in her pack and looked at it. She didn't need to take everything with her as she went exploring. She had to come back to the ruins to meet whomever Nellen organized for her food, so the ruins would make a good base. She would phone Nellen at the shop later.

Although she wanted to keep the watering can, she knew she couldn't take it on her travels. The fountain would make a good home for it. That, she decided, was a fitting place even if the water rusted it away. She put the urn, her water bottle, some food and the few valuables she had into her small shoulder bag. The rest of her things she left in her pack and placed it on a ledge.

Going back down wasn't as easy as going up. She slipped with the stones and found herself running, unable to stop until the ground levelled out. Slumping forward, hands on hips, she gasped for air and coughed out the dust that puffed up around her. She almost felt the smarting of skinned knees and arms, but she hadn't fallen!

She headed for the other side of the ruins and found some names etched into the rock. Some even had dates, Das 1892, Erus 1950, but Deerg wasn't among them. A picture had been scratched deep into the rock as well, but it was too weathered to decipher.

Haras picked up a sharp rock and began scratching her own name. It didn't scratch as easily as she thought it would, so she didn't persist. Maybe she would come back later and work on it.

She spotted a simple white wooden cross, in surprisingly good condition and looked for a name, but there was none. Someone had weeding around it, and placed a single rose across the soil. It was dead too. She turned full circle but couldn't see anyone, or any other evidence of people.

Haras lingered as though being there would bring some answers. She was thinking of her own mother … again. A few mouthfuls from her water bottle washed the thoughts away and she began to think of ancient paths. She couldn't see any evidence of an ancient anything. She headed towards the fountain.

The trickle of water sparkled in the morning sun like little diamonds: dancing light. Haras part filled her water bottle and added some of the protein-enriched powder she'd bought as a meal substitute. After a good shake, the smoothie thickened up and she enjoyed her rehydrated breakfast. She washed the bottle, refilled it, and packed it away, the warning from her dream running through her mind.

Seeing a tall flat rock, she placed the watering can on it. *More artwork on a plinth.* She stood back to admire it. *Another photo subject. Perfect!*

The fountain had a few smooth flat stones around the base and Haras began looking for more. They resembled the stones she'd seen in a picture of an ancient Roman road. An hour passed and Haras decided they were the only ones, so she followed the muddied water to the trees. The water didn't seem to go beyond them. She heeded the warning in her dream and went back to the fountain.

"What secrets do you hold?" she said to the hole in the cross, speculating about where the water pipe was under the ground. She looked past the fountain to a group of larger boulders, squared like quarried rock. Some lay as though toppled from a great height. Others looked like mushroom-shaped towers growing up from the ground. A path, perhaps made by the goats, forked to the left and the right. Renner's words flicked through her mind. *The right path is the right one.* She chose it.

The path ended before a heap of giant stones. A worn grey tree leaned over as if it had tried to climb them. Its' dead roots wrapped down over the stones like lion legs. *How strange. The tree is moulded by what it clings to.*

She took her sunglasses off for a better look and played with the words. *A strong hold becomes a stronghold … a bold hold shapes the holder.*

Haras wanted to see if the path continued beyond them. Climbing was hard work. She wished she had lizard hands to grip the wall before her. Should she give up and go back? She wasn't sure. Some boulders lay on their side. She began climbing them, and reached the top. There she saw another wall, only this one was man-made. Was it enclosing a garden? She could make out a rectangular shape, yet if it was a garden, there were no signs that anyone had tended it for years, not even the goats.

Something caught her eye at the base of the wall. It wasn't a rock, but clay pottery partly buried in the soil. She picked her way over the remaining rocks for a closer look.

That's strange. A watering can and now a flower-pot.

She bent to inspect it. The clay pot was broken. She scraped the soil away from its base and lifted it out, then looked for a good place to photograph it. Nothing inspired her. The place was too overgrown with tall, dead weeds, nearly waist high. The place looked as broken as the flower-pot.

A slight breeze rippled through the weeds and Haras caught sight of a few cherry tomatoes. They clung to spindly, dry stalks. She pushed her way through the undergrowth and picked them, enjoying their sweetness.

Flower-pot in hand, Haras decided to follow the wall. She whacked the dry weeds with her walking stick and stomped on them to make a path. The dry smell filled her mind as well as her nose and she soon changed her mind. It was too overgrown. She was about to go back, when she saw a low wall through the undergrowth. It wasn't made of shaped stone blocks, just large rocks. She pushed through the mess of weeds and found some gravel against the wall. It was too dry even for weeds. There she saw a strange sight.

"A stone man!"

The sound of her own voice made her laugh. A rock had been split by a tree root. It looked just like a man smoking a pipe. His mouth turned down and even the pipe drooped. As Haras studied him, his despondent look took hold of her too. She shook it off and placed the flower-pot beside him.

Seeing a few dry white flowers, she picked them and arranged them in the pot.
"Some flowers to cheer you up, Mr Stone-man." She laughed again.

His face remained as stony as ever.

Haras wanted to keep the pot and the flowers, but his heavy face reminded her that she could only travel light. "Well Mr Stone-man, I think this pot belongs here with you." She took a photo of the scene. *A sad man in a sad place …*

Haras swatted an insect and sat down with her back against the wall. This place was like a secret garden. If she owned the place, she wouldn't have let it get into this state! She took her shoulder bag off. It was time to eat.

The Stone-man continued to smoke his pipe while Haras debated whether she should look for an entrance to the garden, or go back. It had taken her half a day to get this far. She decided to go back.

The trampled grass made it easy to find her way to the boulders she'd climbed. With effort, she climbed one and stood high, unsure how she was going to get down. Nothing was familiar, yet it must've been the boulder she'd climber before.

Leaping down dislodged a few pebbles and they rolled down the bank. Haras placed her hands on a large boulder to steady herself. She didn't want to cause an avalanche.

It wasn't long before she found the path. She wasn't lost!

Reaching the place where the path forked Haras took the left one. It was still too early to go back to the ruins for the night. Her phone beeped, signalling a text message and she fumbled for it as she continued down the path. A sudden movement caught her eye - a snake? She turned back to check it out. Something moved again. *A lizard?* Below it were shoe prints, two faint indents. It wasn't only the goats who'd been on this path. She placed one foot in the print. It was made by a bigger boot than hers.

Haras furrowed her brows and pursed her lips. Someone had been in the area. What had they been doing? Was it the same person who had weeded the wooden cross? Had the prints been made at that time? They were hard and dry, so maybe not. She poked around with her stick, waving a patch of long grasses back and forwards. There were no other prints.

Haras turned back to her phone, but before she could read the message, the ground rumbled as though a big truck was driving past. A few pebbles slid past her feet. Haras regretted trying the left path.

The earth growled, low and deep. Suddenly and violently it rocked her off her feet. She dropped the walking stick. Her phone went flying. The earth was rolling up toward her. A boulder crashed down the bank. She couldn't stand, or stop herself from sliding backwards after it. She screamed as she fell through a gaping hole between the rocks and realised she *treasured* her life.

Chapter 19

Running water? Haras licked her dry lips. A drop splashed against her cheek and she opened her eyes. It was dark and cool, but there was sand in her mouth. It was gritty and she tried to spit it out. Where was she? What was she doing here?

Haras tried to take a deep breath but her chest hurt so badly. She took half breaths and tried to sit up but the pain was so intense she thought she would faint. She lay on her back, very still, taking shallow breaths.

Another drop of water splashed near her mouth, Haras licked at it. Her face was wet. Had she been crying? Her legs were wet. Water was running past them. How long had she had been lying there? Hours? Days?

An earthquake. She'd been in an earthquake! She tried to sit up again, but couldn't. The movement caused pain so intense she couldn't tell where it was. Her throat was so dry, but all she could do was open her mouth for the drip. Sometimes it landed near her tongue, but mostly it trickled down her face with a tear. Everything was so quiet she could hear her heart racing.

No-one will find you here! The words of her dream flashed into her mind and she believed them. She knew many people cried out to God when they couldn't save themselves, so she did too.

"Help me get out of here and I will believe in you!" A shaft of light streamed in through a cavity in the rock. More tears trickled down her checks.

"Jesus, help me!" Her voice echoed in the dark cavern, drowning out her heartbeat, but not the pain.

Something moved. She focused hard to see what it was. It had the shape of a large lizard. It moved into the light and sat watching her. A palpable calmness came into her heart. She watched the lizard watching her and for a moment, the pain eased, but then she moved and the pain returned. She closed her eyes and drifted in and out of sleep, waking whenever she moved.

"Down here!" Was she dreaming?

"She's down here."

Someone *was* calling out. She wasn't dreaming. A tear pricked her eyes, then ran down her cheek, but she couldn't talk. Someone had found her! A head of dark curly hair blocked the shaft of light. Was it the man from Klat's store? He was talking to someone.

"Renner. She's here!" The young man climbed down through the light. He knelt beside her, plying her with questions. She couldn't speak. She didn't want to speak. It was too hard to think.

"My back ... can't move ..."

"It's her back. She can't move," he yelled up to someone.

"Don't try to move her, could make it much worse."

"... thirsty ... water."

"She's thirsty. Can I give her some water?"

"A little water should be ok. Not too much."

"Ok."

He undid a leather flask attached to his belt, removed the lid and placed it to her lips. She wanted to drink more than the small mouthful of water that passed through her lips.

"Not too much. May not be safe for her."

Was that Renner's voice?

"You're going to be all right," the man beside her said.

Haras heard the kindness in his tone and it hurt her heart. She closed her eyes. She didn't want him to see her tears. He continued speaking quietly. Haras couldn't make out what he was saying, but it calmed her, like her gran's hug.

The helicopter won't be long ... but it was. It seemed like forever before someone fastened a neck brace on. Someone else strapped her onto a stretcher. She closed her eyes as she was lifted out, out into the light.

It was too bright. She closed her eyes again and wished they would put her down. It was too bumpy! She felt sick. She was thirsty and tired. Relieved, but tired. She felt the wind from the helicopter blades ... She was on her way to hospital.

Chapter 20

Sleep was what Haras wanted, but light from a small torch shone in her eyes. She didn't want to look at it.

"Open your eyes!" The command shocked her eyes open. Haras just wanted to go to sleep. Too many questions she didn't want to answer.

"What day is it?"

"The weekend?"

They slid something under her back for an X-ray … and then the doctor was back again speaking too fast.

"Fractured rib. There it is." One of the doctors pointed it out on the X-ray.

"TBI?"

"CAT scan?"

"Maybe."

Haras relaxed back, thankful the medication in the drip was working. All but one of the doctors left. He sat at a table with his back to her, writing. Every so often he turned and looked briefly at her then resumed writing.

A group of nurses came in. They wheeled her down the corridor and into another room. One nurse slid a toilet pan under her lower back. The pain was so intense. Haras screamed. "Take it out. Take it out!"

Another doctor came in. "Where does it hurt?"

Haras didn't know. The pain had been too intense. He helped her roll over and gave her several injections down her ribs.

"Some people never feel pain again after these injections," the doctor said.

Haras hoped she'd be one of them. She was still lying on her stomach when the doctor left. She panicked. She didn't know how to roll onto her back. She had to be on her back. She wouldn't be able to breathe. Was the doctor going to leave her there?

Fighting the panic, Haras called out. She waited. Had anyone heard her? She felt utterly alone in the hospital room, unable to move. She couldn't reach the button to call a nurse ... then the doctor was standing beside her bed.

"How do I roll over?"

"You just roll over."

Haras couldn't even think of how this was done, so she asked him to help her and he did.

That night, after a CAT scan, as Haras fell asleep, her body felt like an intensely painful cage. She felt separated from her body. She was just a ball inside it, but there was another ball of solid light beside her. From somewhere inside, she heard the word 'Jesus.'

Haras didn't sleep for long. It wasn't encouraged. Nurses kept coming in, checking the drip, checking her vital statistics, shining a torch in her eyes. Haras wanted some of her own questions answered. What was TBI? What did the CAT scan show? She couldn't see her shoulder bag. Where were her things? Her phone?

The following day Haras was told the scan hadn't shown any obvious Traumatic Brain Injury. She was also told that Renner had called a friend after the earthquake. They'd gone together to check that she was okay. When they found the old walking stick near the opening in the cavern and saw her hat, they knew she wasn't, and when they found her, Renner phoned the emergency services while his much-younger friend climbed in to help her. They had lifted her out and flown her by helicopter to the hospital.

Haras stewed over the events. She wanted to roll over but couldn't. Her things! Where were her things?

"Don't worry! We advise patients not to keep valuables with them in the hospital," a nurse said.

Another nurse came in. "Renner's taken them for safe keeping. He has your travel details and contacted the Embassy. The Embassy contacted your insurance company and us. Don't worry!"

No matter how many times they said it, Haras couldn't seem to say what she wanted to say and she couldn't stop worrying. She didn't *know* Renner and everyone seemed to think she did.

Many other questions came into her mind as she lay in the hospital bed. Had God really answered her cry for help? Would she have been found anyway? How did she know the ball of light was Jesus—?

"Time for a shower."

The curt command of a nurse jarred Haras. As she bent to help Haras into a wheelchair, Haras felt herself pulling away from the smell of stale cigarettes. The nurse wheeled her to the showers, still connected to a drip, then helped her to stand. A patient called from the adjoining shower and left her to wash herself. Haras felt as though she was going to faint, and anxiously called out to the nurse. She didn't answer. Haras called again.

"Just bend over," the nurse replied.

"I can't," Haras said and fear clutched at her chest.

"No that's right you can't," the nurse replied, but she didn't come to help.

Haras panicked. She was going to faint! Instead, she cried out to Jesus for help again. This time she felt a warm sensation come into her head that strengthened her. She didn't faint.

Back in bed Haras forgot the indifference of the nurse as she saw a bouquet of blue and white flowers on her dresser. The nurse saw her looking at them and picked up a card. They were from Renner.

Haras felt comforted. Renner had given her flowers and he wasn't even a close friend. Would he visit her soon? Would she get her things back? She wished she knew someone in Y'kahs. Tears rolled down her checks as she drifted into sleep.

"Leave them here," she heard the nurse say.

Haras opened her eyes and saw Renner place a small bag of apples on the table and turn.

"Hello." Renner smiled and sat down again. "For a moment I thought I would have to leave before you woke." Even his eyes were smiling and Haras found herself smiling weakly as she woke up. It was the first time in a long time, she'd smiled, or at least, that was what it felt like. His kind eyes drew her away from the anxious thoughts.

"Thank you for the flowers, and thank you for helping me." Haras felt as though she was always thanking him.

"I'm here to help," he said as he patted her hand. Tears pricked her eyes again but were soon gone as he placed her shoulder bag on the bed.

"You may want us to continue keeping your things safe while you're in hospital," he said.

Haras relaxed. "Thanks." She looked into her bag. Nothing seemed to be missing.

"Did you see my phone? I dropped it in the earthquake."

"No, I didn't see it."

Haras's thoughts began to wander. Renner must have noticed because he stood, promising to come again and Haras drifted off to sleep again.

She woke to the tap-tap of high-heeled shoes. She saw them first; very high heels. The lady wearing them was dressed in a black dress suit and white blouse. *Government office worker?*

The lady introduced herself. She was from the Embassy.

"We contacted the hospital as soon as we heard about your accident."

Haras had already forgotten her name.

"We spoke with Renner. Some of the staff here know him. Used to be rostered on to visit the sick, I've been told, until he moved away. Is there anyone else you want us to contact back home?

"Yes, Ahsha." She couldn't remember Ahsha's number … now that was strange. Probably shock from the accident.

"Can you please contact Ahsha. Her contact details are in my bag. Renner has my bag."

The lady didn't stay long but left her card. Haras relaxed. She wasn't royalty, but everyone was treating her as though she was.

No sooner had she departed than another visitor arrived. Haras saw his dark curly head above a box arrangement of pink and white flowers.

"Hi, Haras." He placed the flowers on the windowsill.

"Hi."

"I'm Nen." He held out his hand, and Haras took it. He squeezed it gently and briefly.

"I helped Renner get you into the helicopter. You probably don't remember. Your eyes were closed."

"Thanks." She looked at the flowers. "They're lovely. Thanks for helping me."

"Glad to. I was going to drive Renner out to pick you up or deliver some food ... Easier in my 4WD."

Nen ran his hand through his hair and Haras wanted to say something, but nothing came to mind, except how long his eyelashes were.

"Anyway, I can't stay long." He pushed the black cuff of his shirt back and looked at his gold watch. "Visiting time's nearly over. I just wanted to make sure you were okay."

Haras found her voice again. "Thanks. I'm pretty sore, but the medication helps."

He smiled and Haras was surprised by the kindness she saw in his brown eyes.

She smiled back, and then lowered her eyes.

"Visiting time's up." A nurse walked in and hurried Nen towards the door, where he turned.

"Bye," he said and smiled again.

"Bye and thanks," Haras said.

Nen's smile lingered in her mind.

Chapter 21

"Feeling better today?"

Haras looked up, glad to see a different nurse. This one was all smiles as she read Haras's chart, and her soft brown eyes sparkled as they met hers.

"I see you have eaten."

The nurse spoke slowly with an accent that made it difficult for Haras to follow.

"Yes, a little," Haras said.

The nurse put the chart back and looked towards the door. "Your friend phoned," she said putting her hand to her ear to get her message across. "Ah-something. We did not wake you."

"Ahsha?"

"Yes. Maybe that is it," the nurse said. She pointed to the door. "Your grandparents are here."

"My what?" Haras looked towards the door. Her heart skipped a beat.

"Grandparents." The nurse nodded as Renner walked in.

"Oh, you mean Renner."

The nurse nodded and Renner nodded back to her.

"Hello, Ono. How's your mother?" he said.

Haras looked from Renner to the nurse. They knew each other?

"She is well, thank you," the nurse replied.

"She misses her apartment, but has made a friend in the rest home. She has everything she needs and she is close for me to visit. Thank you again for visiting her. It meant a lot to us both."

"That's good news." Renner smiled and Haras noticed the warmth in his expression as he turned to look at her.

"Haras, this is my wife Megagem." He stepped back and Haras saw an elegant lady behind him.

Megagem walked towards the bed like a queen and Haras half-expected her to sit down and wave like one too. She did sit down, but didn't wave. She gave Haras a broad lipstick smile revealing perfect white teeth.

Surely not her own, not at her age. It surprised Haras to see such a grandmotherly welcome in her face. Megagem reminded Haras of Emme.

"Not her grandparents?" the nurse asked.

Megagem and Renner laughed. "No."

The nurse smiled and left.

Megagem took off her wide brimmed hat revealing a mass of grey and white curls. She placed the hat on the bed; white on white.

"How are you feeling now?"

Haras gave a weak smile.

"Improving, thanks."

"The ruins aren't the safest of places at the best of times ..."

Happy-chatty like Emme too, but not as soft and spongy—.

Renner put her shoulder bag on the bed to reassure her it was safe with them. She rummaged through. Everything was still there!

"The Embassy contacted your friend Ahsha and gave her our phone number," Renner said. "She phoned us and sends her love. She's praying for you, and so is her mother and her church."

"We are too." Megagem said. "Is there no-one here to care for you when you get out?"

"No. I've been looking for my father, but he doesn't know I exist—"

"Our home used to be a bed and breakfast. We have plenty of room if you'd like to stay with us when you get out of hospital," Megagem said.

"We have an open home," Renner said. "We'd love you to come and stay with us, free of charge, so don't worry about a thing." His eyes were soft, his smile tender. Haras bit down on her bottom lip to stop it from quivering.

"We can collect you from hospital when it's time for you to leave … that is, if you would like to come. No need to decide yet. Think about it and let us know."

Haras found her thoughts alternating between the positives of staying with them and the possible dangers of taking them up on their offer. She thanked them for their kindness, and although she thought she would accept it, she didn't say so. She wanted to get to know them better first.

As they left, a nurse came into the room with a phone. "Call for you."

It was Ahsha. Haras felt tearful just hearing her voice. She told them about Renner and Megagem.

"They seemed to bring peace into the room with them."

"Yes, they do sound lovely. The Embassy gave me their number and I phoned them. Mum spoke to them for some time too. They told me they are happy to look after you when you get out of hospital. They do hospital visits, so they know what you might need when you get out. They are Christians too. So that's perfect."

"Christians?"

"Yes."

Haras wanted to tell Ahsha about what had happened when she called out to Jesus in the shower, but didn't know how to explain it. "They said something about an open home. Have you heard of that?"

"No, but I think they mean they are happy to invite strangers into their home. They like to provide hospitality like the ancients did."

"Ancients?"

"People in biblical times. It was part of their culture to welcome strangers."

"Oh."

"I'm glad you're awake. I'll phone again tomorrow, Okay? You sure you don't need anything else?"

"Not at the moment. Thanks, Ahsha. It's so good to hear your voice."

The next day Renner and Megagem came again and Haras thought Megagem was like her name, a real gem. When she bent over and kissed her goodbye, on her forehead, Haras remembered her mother's bedtime kiss, the kiss she'd given her every night when she was little. Megagem's kiss had a similar effect. It left her deeply calmed. It also left Haras wondering if Megagem thought she was younger than she was. This might be her last year as a teenager, but she certainly didn't feel like a child!

After the first visit, Megagem began coming alone. Each time she brought some little thing to cheer Haras up. There were new pyjamas, flowers, the clothes Haras had been wearing, now washed and folded into a carry bag, chocolates and more flowers. On a handcrafted card she'd written, "*In your distress you called and I rescued you* (Psalm 81:7)."

Haras read the words when visiting time was over. She rubbed her eyes with her palms and reread them. The words spoke assurance to her that God had heard her cry and orchestrated her rescue. How amazing that out of all the words she could have written, Megagem had chosen to write those words.

It was an age going through the days, and Haras looked forward to being well enough to leave, but when the doctor finally announced she could go home, she wasn't ready.

"I don't have a "home," Haras said. "I still can't get in and out of bed without help."

"You've had more days than broken ribs are allowed. Even if your insurance company does agree to pay for you to stay longer, physiotherapy is what you need now, not a hospital bed."

Haras wanted to tell him she'd only been able to get out of bed by herself when she pressed the bed button, which moved her into a sitting position. When it was flat she couldn't get out, but he left as abruptly as he had arrived and Haras cried out to God in panic.

Impatient and brisk, a nurse came into the room, her stride wafting fresh cigarette smell throughout the room.

"You need to get ready to go," she said and pulled the blanket down. "Time to leave the hospital."

Haras shivered.

"Normally it wouldn't matter how long you stay, as long as the insurance company pays, but there's been a serious accident. Bus collided with a car. We need all the beds we can get. People tend to get better quicker at home anyway." She wrote something on Haras's chart. "Is there someone you can phone to come and get you?"

Haras hesitated. There was no-one but Renner and Megagem. She still couldn't get out of bed without help, so she couldn't go to the hotel, and she didn't have her shoulder bag.

Haras silently cried out to God, "What am I going to do?" Immediately Emme's words popped into her mind. *Don't be afraid.*

Nurse Ono walked in and took the chart. "So you're going home today Haras?" she said. "Are you going to stay with Renner and Megagem? They were so good to my mother when she had a stroke. From time to time, they take in people who stay for some months. You'll be in good hands with them."

Haras felt reassured. Everyone seemed to know Renner and Megagem and no-one had a bad word about them, not even Ahsha. Accepting Renner and Megagem's offer seemed the right thing to do – the right path.

"Yes. Will you phone them for me please?" The words popped out of her mouth before Haras could stop them.

Nurse Ono left to phone Renner and came back a few minutes later. Renner and Megagem were on their way.

Chapter 22

"Is someone coming for you?" A nurse asked as she entered the room. Haras looked up. She hadn't seen this nurse before. The nurse fussed around the room and Haras felt pressured to leave.

"Yes. They're on their way."

The nurse left. Haras worried as the minutes ticked by. Had something happened to Renner and Megagem? She listened for their steps, but only heard the soft pad of nurse's outside her room. One was approaching. *What now?*

The nurse helped Haras to get ready and left her sitting in the bedside chair. Haras closed her eyes and waited.

"Hello."

Haras looked up. It was the lady she'd sat next to on the flight over. Izzi.

"Well, don't look so surprised!"

Haras closed her mouth. "What are you doing here?"

Izzi handed Haras a box of soft centred chocolates and a card. "I could say the same to you. I read about your accident in the newspaper, and thought I'd visit you. You said you didn't know anyone here, so I thought you might like a visit."

"Thanks, but you nearly missed me. I'm about to leave. Do you want to sit down?"

Haras pointed to the spare chair and Izzi turned it to face Haras. She lifted her long hair, before sitting down. As she crossed her legs, Haras admired her strappy stiletto heels. The straps ended just below her knees.

"Nice aren't they?" Izzi said. "Crocodile skin. From Paris, although the crocodile probably came from Australia." She gave a short laugh.

Haras smiled. "A perfect match for your dress."

"Paris too – stopped there a few weeks before coming here. So, you survived an earthquake?"

"Yes. I didn't think I'd ever be found, but I was."

Izzi nodded. "Indeed. I'm pleased you're okay, and I'm pleased I didn't miss you. Oh, by the way, I did ask my friend about your family. They didn't recognize the name."

"Thanks for asking," Haras said.

"What are you doing next?"

"I'm going to stay with a couple, who have a bed and breakfast place. They've offered to look after me while I recover."

"Oh, that's great."

"I'm waiting for them. They're coming to pick me up."

"So you don't need a ride? I was about to offer to take you."

"Thanks, but they're on their way."

"Well, I must be too. There's a photographic exhibition I want to see before I fly out tonight."

"Oh."

Izzi stood and straightened her tight skirt. "When I'm back in Y'kahs, maybe we can meet up for a drink or something. What's the name of the bed and breakfast?"

"Akiiki," Haras said.

"That should be easy to remember. It means friend. Well, I hope you find everything you're looking for here, and lots of friends." She laughed and turned towards the door.

"Thanks for thinking of me, Izzi."

"My pleasure. Don't get up. I'll see myself out." She laughed again and was gone as quickly as she'd come.

Haras opened the card and read it. Izzi had written her name, and an email address, but nothing else. Haras closed it and closed her eyes again.

It was nearly two hours before Megagem appeared at the door. Renner was right behind her.

They carried her things to the car and opened the door for her. She wasn't sure how to sit down into the car without hurting. She sat down on the seat then swung her legs in. Renner closed the door.

The ride to their home was almost more than Haras could bear. She felt every bump and had a hard time fighting back the tears. At last they arrived.

"Akiiki. That means friend." Megagem said and pointed to the bed and breakfast sign on the fence.

Haras noticed the 'No Vacancy' sign hanging beneath it.

The gates opened automatically and Renner drove the car in and parked outside a garage at the side of the house. Megagem helped Haras out and she walked carefully along a path that led to the front door of their home.

Blessed are they believing they are blessed. Haras read the palindrome on a plaque beside the door, but was too weary even to think about it.

Megagem led her to a room. The bed covers had been turned down ready for her. The pillows were embroidered with small white roses. It was a lovely touch.

"Do you need help with anything?" Megagem asked. Haras needed help to undo her boots and lie back into the bed. Megagem was only too pleased to fuss over her. Haras crossed her arms and Megagem placed her arm behind Haras' back. She took Haras's weight and lowered her onto the fresh white sheets. Haras relaxed carefully into the bed and signed deeply. The bed was everything she wanted. It felt like home.

Megagem opened the wardrobe and handed Haras her shoulder bag.

"Don't worry about a thing." She rang a little bell on the bedside table and placed it on the bed where Haras could reach it.

"Use the bell if you need help getting up again, or if you need anything else."

Megagem left the room and Haras checked her things. She relaxed further into the pillow and was soon dozing, still holding tightly to her things. She woke when Megagem appeared with a rice meal on a bed tray.

"You look a lot better now. That sleep has put a little colour back in your face."

"I feel a lot better, thanks. The car-ride didn't agree with me."

Megagem helped Haras to sit and fluffed up her pillows to support her back before leaving again.

Haras enjoyed the meal and thanked Megagem when she returned for the tray.

"Would you like to use the phone?"

"I would, but not right now. Ahsha, will still be asleep. I need to buy a phone so I can text her."

"Well, in the meantime, if you want to borrow Renner's phone, you can text her on that. Do you want me to get it for you?"

"That would be great. Thanks."

Megagem took the meal tray and soon returned with the phone and a small address book. She opened it. "I have Ahsha's phone number here," she said as she handed it to Haras. She left the room.

Haras texted a short message to Ahsha to let her know she'd borrowed Renner and Megagem's phone, and was staying with them. She smiled and noticed she wasn't anxious. Someone was singing. Was it Megagem?

The singing stopped and Megagem appeared at the door. "Let me know when you need to use the bathroom and I'll help you up," she said.

"Might as well go now."

Megagem pulled back the bed linen and Haras swung her legs, one at a time over the edge. With Megagem's help she was able to stand. She didn't need help to walk to the ensuite or to go looking for Megagem. She found her in the kitchen. Megagem pulled a matching chair out from beneath the wood table top.

"Thanks," Haras said. She ran her hand over the smooth polished ash timber top. "What a lovely table, and the kitchen they all look so new."

"Thanks. We've only just finished renovating it. So much more room now. We took out a wall." She pointed to where it had been.

Haras nodded. "I like the open-plan look and the white look."

Megagem ran her hand over the white granite bench-top. "I do enjoy it. I love island benches. It makes cooking preparation and entertaining so much easier."

"Yes. I have one at home, too," Haras said. "Do you do much entertaining?"

"Not as much as I used to, but Renner and I often have friends over. What about you?"

"Ahsha comes over for dinner most weeks. I've been too busy working and studying to do much entertaining."

Renner poked his head around the door. "You're looking a better colour."

Haras touched her face. "Thanks. I feel a lot better. And thanks for the loan of your phone."

"Any time. Just ask."

They chatted for some time and Megagem helped Haras back into bed.

As she lay there, Haras thought about what body part she had to move, to try and get out of bed without help. First, she needed to move the left leg so that it was hanging over the edge of the bed. Next, she had to move the other leg and roll over and up. It took her a few days of concentrated practicing before she could get up by herself without much pain. Once up, she couldn't stay up for too long, as she would begin to feel as though her legs would give way.

Recovering was easier out of hospital, just as the nurse had said. No more nurses waking her up in the night. No more nurses at her beck and call either, but Megagem was only too happy to come running. She was a real *gem* and never too busy to help her.

Haras valued her independence. She didn't want to bother Megagem too much, so she was glad when she was finally able get up without help. After that, she started reducing the pain medication.

Megagem did many little things to make Haras feel welcome and at home. There were always fresh flowers in a vase on the dresser, water in a jug beside her bed, and the kind of food she liked to eat. She treated Haras as she would her own granddaughter, and it felt just right to Haras.

On her way back to bed one day, Haras caught a glimpse of herself in a mirror. It didn't look like her at all. How long was it since she'd looked at herself in a mirror? She stood in front of it refreshing her memory and remembered her family photo. Where was it? It wasn't in her bag. Surely she hadn't left it on the ledge with her other things in the ancient ruins.

Chapter 23

Now and then Renner and Megagem came in and chatted with Haras. Two chairs had been placed near the bed, and Haras enjoyed their company and the chance to learn their native language. Megagem was an excellent teacher. She said she'd had lots of practice on their guests, but Haras was definitely a fast learner. Haras doubted it, but was pleased Megagem thought so. It made her feel a bit special to them. They treated her so well, sometimes Haras pretended they were her own grandparents.

After she'd been there a couple of weeks, Renner said to her, "Do you know you have a heavenly Father who loves you very much?"

Haras was taken aback. She couldn't picture God as her father. What was a father really like? Hers was missing. She believed God enough to speak to Him a few times, but the idea of Him as her father wasn't something she liked.

"What do you mean? What does that mean?"

"Have you ever heard *The Lord's Prayer*?" he asked.

"Yes, but I don't know it. My Gran used to pray it sometimes."

"*Our father*, that's how it begins. Jesus called God, 'Dad,' and that's how close our heavenly Father wants to be with us."

Haras tried to imagine God sitting in a chair beside Renner. "How do you get to be that close?" Haras asked.

"How do you get close to anyone?"

Haras thought about all the things one did to get to know someone.

Finally, Renner said, "God enjoys conversation." After a long pause he continued. "He likes to talk to His children and listen to them too. Not just occasionally but every day."

"What do you talk to God about?"

"We dialogue throughout the day about most things. I say 'Good morning' when I wake up and we chat, mostly silently, about the weather, about things that need doing, about problems."

"There is so much to thank Him for too," Megagem said.

Haras could imagine Megagem chatting with God and having a lot to thank Him for. She was chatty.

"Would you like us to chat with Him now?" Megagem asked.

Haras stared at her toes poking up under the covers. She curled them under, and twisted a sheet between her fingers. She wasn't sure she wanted to—could, out loud, but she nodded.

"We're glad we can call you our father," Megagem prayed. "You are the best father we could ever have. You're always here for us and as close as a prayer."

Renner continued. "Thank you for the blessing Haras is to us. Let her experience the deep love you have for all your children. Satisfy her Father, and heal her ..."

As Haras listened, her eyes brimmed with tears. She'd never heard anything like this before. She'd never felt anything like this before. It was as though God was wrapping her up in a blanket of love, and she found she had a little thankfulness inside, for God too.

"Thank you," she prayed in an almost audible voice and reached for a tissue to wipe her eyes.

As the days passed, she became a little bolder in praying aloud with them, and thought of more things she could thank God for.

A few people came, stayed overnight and left, which made the days passed more quickly than Haras imagined they would, and after Renner gave her a Bible to read, the days merged into one another. She thought it would be nice to keep her photo inside it, but she forgot to ask Renner about it. When she did remember both Renner and Megagem were out. They never seemed to be around to ask when she thought of it.

Two weeks after receiving the Bible, they were. She was sitting on the veranda when they returned from a shopping trip with the phone she'd paid them to get. It reminded her of the things she had left on the ledge in the ancient ruins. She asked Renner if anyone had found them.

He looked puzzled and shook his head. "We checked inside the ruins, when we were looking for you, but didn't see a tent, or sleeping bag or anything else there. The only thing we saw that seemed a bit out of place was a gold pan. Looked like someone had cleaned it."

"That sounds like the one I found," Haras said.

The photo's whereabouts was a mystery, and Haras worried about it. The last time she remembered looking at the photo was at Klat's Store. Had she left the photo there? Surely, she didn't leave it with the tent.

"I'll ask about it the next time I'm in the store." Renner said and patted Megagem on the arm. "That's where we get Megagem's favourite chocolate cakes."

Megagem chuckled and patted Renner's arm back. "Is it my imagination Haras, or are you developing an addiction as well? I never have to twist anyone's arm to eat them!"

Haras wiggled in the chair. "You can add my name to the list of people in this household who like them," she said.

They all laughed.

"Why not give the store a call? You could try your new phone out." Megagem said. "Ask about your photo and order some cakes at the same time."

Renner stood. "I'll get the number for you."

Haras followed Renner into the lounge and took the card he handed her. She phoned, but was disappointed. No-one at the shop that day had seen her photo. She texted Ahsha and Ahsha immediately phoned her back.

"Only got a minute to talk," she said. "Breakfast time here. I'm running late. Is this your new phone?"

"Yep. Now I might be able to catch you at lunch or morning tea again."

"Great. Talk later then."

Haras was looking forward to talking. She hadn't liked to borrow Renner's phone too often. Ahsha had rung a few times on her lunch break and it had been great hearing her voice. Somehow, it helped Haras feel more at home and she was beginning to feel as if that was where she was. She hadn't forgotten her mission, to find her father. It was important, but it didn't worry her as much as before. She had found her heavenly Father and a comfortable home in which to rest a while, and she felt somewhat satisfied, more than she'd ever felt before.

Haras smiled as she remembered telling Ahsha she'd found her heavenly Father. Ahsha had been over the moon. "You've found family," she'd said. "We have the same Father, so now you've got a sister as well - me. And you have a travelling companion. We're both travelling in the same place, God's kingdom."

Chapter 24

Daily Bible reading became a habit and two months after receiving the Bible, Haras was reading the book of Jeremiah when a verse seemed to light up. *This is what the LORD says: 'Stand in the beaten track and see; ask for the ancient paths, ask where the good way is, and walk in it, and you will find rest.'*

Haras was excited. The ancient paths were the *good way*! She repeated the words in her mind. *Ask for the ancient paths; ask where the good way is.* She did. First, she asked Jesus, and Renner's words about the right path being the right path popped into her mind. She rushed out to ask him about the *good way* too.

Renner wasn't quick to answer her. She waited. Was he consulting *their* heavenly Father?

"You need to ask your heavenly Father that. He will teach you what is good for you and lead you in the best paths."

Later he told her to read the words of Jesus in John 14. When she did, it was as though Jesus was speaking directly to her. *Don't let your hearts be agitated.* She knew she was often troubled and harassed, like her name. *You believe in God …* yes she did, now she did. B*elieve in me.*

Haras asked God about what she was to believe and as she continued reading she caught a glimpse.

I am the way … Don't you know me … I will not leave you as orphans …

It was as though the passage had been written especially for her. She wasn't an orphan any more. She had a heavenly Father, and Jesus was the way, the good path. Did following Him mean walking on or in ancient paths?

Haras looked at the word *in* and knew she wanted her feet in that path.

Ask!

Haras asked, and immediately knew, she had a part to play. How was she to stop herself from being anxious?

Ask!

She did and again immediately, she knew. She let her own thoughts lead her towards anxiety. She would find rest from the anxiety if she asked, and then did what Jesus said. She didn't want her own thoughts leading her down her own path. She wanted them to *go in* those ancient paths, where Jesus led them.

Ask!

Again, Haras asked and a deep peace came into her. She felt as though she was sitting enveloped by a tangible presence of rest. She was in those ancient paths. She was in that rest. Now, she always wanted to be found in it and on it, not on her own path, following her own thoughts. God's way was better.

She looked over at the urn. It referred to one ancient path. Was Jesus the ancient path of the urn? She put the Bible down and picked up the urn. The lid still rattled. What was inside?

Haras took it with her and went in search of Renner. She found him in the kitchen.

"I've found the ancient paths. Renner, I've found them."

Renner laughed. "Are you sure the Ancient Path didn't find you?"

Haras stopped.

Renner chuckled. "You look worried."

"Do I?" Haras beamed and held up the urn. "I'm curious, very curious. I knocked my urn over and the lid was dented. It's rattled ever since. Do you have anything I could use to prise the top open.

"Let me see." Renner wiped his hands on a towel. He took the lid and turned it over. "I see. I see what you mean. It does sound as though something's inside. But you might damage the lid by prising it open."

"I don't mind taking the risk."

"Then come with me. I have some tools that might do the job."

Renner grinned and Haras followed him out to the garage. She watched as Renner carefully used a few different tools to open the lid.

"Well, well!" he exclaimed when he finally found a way to open it "A secret chamber for ancient treasure!"

Haras put out her hand. She couldn't wait to see it. "What is it? Let me see!"

Renner held out his hand. A silver band held a smooth white stone. A Star of David had been carved into it. Haras turned it over and they both stared. The other side showed a cross and some fish.

"Jewish and early Christian symbols," Renner said. "Odd that it's in an Egyptian urn."

"Looks ancient. Do you think it's older than the urn?" Haras turned it over again.

Renner frowned. "Could be. When I first saw your urn, I was curious and did a bit of research on hieroglyphics and urns. They've only been able to decipher hieroglyphics since the 1800's, according to one internet site I looked up. Hieroglyphics were thought to be the words of gods. Perhaps whoever put the hieroglyphic message on the urn believed it a godly message."

Haras nodded. "Well, it's certainly like the words in the Bible. Jeremiah mentions ancient paths."

Haras saw laughter in Renner's eyes, but he didn't laugh. He pointed at the stone. "This looks older than the urn. It looks like something a Jewish convert might have, but it's rather unusual. Maybe it had been hidden for safe keeping in difficult times."

"Like the last world war," Haras nodded again.

"It's strange." Renner said. "The early Christians and Jews thought cremation was a pagan practice. The Romans practiced it though, so maybe some of the new Christian gentile converts did too, until Constantine outlawed it."

"Maybe I need an archaeologist or some other jewellery expert!" Haras laughed.

Renner laughed as well and gave Haras the stone. "Do you want me to close the lid again or leave it as it is?"

"Leave it open. I'll place the stone back in its little bed. Whoever I get to assess it will need to see where it's been hidden. Thank's Renner. I'll take some photos and see what I can find out."

Haras placed the stone back in its bed. Where was she going to find a suitable and trustworthy expert to shed more light on her mystery? Would someone at the national museum know?

On her way back to her room, a thought stopped her in her tracks. This stone was about the size of the stone heart on her necklace. What if it fitted her necklace?

Haras lay her grandmother's necklace on her bed and could see the engraved stone fitted. It was a perfect match, unlike the heart-shaped stone.

"Wow!" her legs felt wobbly. She sat down and just stared at it. What did it mean? Did her grandmother's birth family hide it in the lid? They must have. The necklace had been hidden in the doll. Why? Why were they separated … in case either the doll or the urn was lost? Both must be valuable.

She made up her mind to visit a jeweller and have the heart removed and the engraved stone attached.

That night Haras phoned Ahsha and told her about the two-sided stone, and what it could mean if Jesus was the ancient path? They ended up with more questions than answers.

Chapter 25

Energy dissipated from Haras, as she let memories from the past linger. The house was unusually quiet. She felt alone.

I will not leave you as orphans.

"I'm not alone." She wasn't an orphan. She had her heavenly Father. It felt good saying it out loud, reminding herself and the world. She imagined many people, ancient people, reading and speaking the same Biblical words. Perhaps it gave them the same feeling of belonging, of being *in* a family. She laughed at the possibility of her thoughts travelling along the same path as the ancients!

Haras smiled as she went looking for Renner. Her ribs didn't hurt, and walking around the house was no longer a problem, but she still couldn't bend over enough to do up her boots. She looked at her slippers glad she didn't have to bend to put them on because Megagem wasn't there to help her put her boots on. She'd gone to an arts and craft meeting at church to teach some young mothers how to make teddy bears. Although there was more freedom among the Christians in Y'kahs, none of the men would be making teddy bears!

Megagem had a lot of shopping to do afterwards, so she hadn't invited Haras to go with her. Haras was pleased. She didn't think she had a motherly streak and didn't particularly like babies, although she didn't say that to Megagem. Having been an only child, she didn't think she had much in common with a lot of the family orientated women, except Megagem, of course. She also wanted to prepare something special for dinner.

Haras found Renner pulling a few weeds in the garden.

"A daily task! They seem to come up overnight." He pointed to some weeds and bent to pull one up. "Better to do a little every day."

Haras agreed. "In the wrong place, any plant is like a weed." She thought she would feel like one among all the mothers.

Renner stood and looked at her. "What's troubling you?"

He had a knack of knowing when she had a question. Once she had asked him how he knew she was troubled about something. He'd replied, "Your face speaks what your heart is feeling."

Haras frowned. "Some people were cold towards me when I mentioned the ancient ruins. Why do they try and discourage people from going there, and why are they called *ancient*? I didn't see much there that suggested *ancient* to me."

Renner's shoulders sagged and his grey checked shirt hung more limply over the waist tie on his dusty fisherman pants. His eyes glazed over as he stared somewhere beyond her. "Some people lost family and friends there in a big earthquake." He took his soiled leather gloves off and shook them. "A group of young people were partying among the ruins. Their death affected most everyone around these parts. Some stopped going to church after that. Some are still angry with God about it and won't talk about it, not to God or anyone else. Perhaps they built a tomb around their grief and are still blaming God."

Haras thought of a family photo she'd seen inside a gardening book. There were two children with Megegem at a park. Renner and Megagem talked often enough about their son and grandchildren, but not their daughter. She asked him softly, "Did you lose anyone?"

"Yes, our daughter was there with the others."

"I'm sorry," Haras said.

"Thank you, Haras. God is always good. Remember that. His people are His treasure, here and in heaven."

"If God treasures me, why didn't He keep me or my mother safe, or the young people?"

Renner bent down and picked up a smooth white stone from the flowerbed, and rolled it over in his hand. "I chose white stones for this flower bed. They remind me that God is going to give those who overcome a new name and write it on a white stone." He paused and his sorrow rubbed off on Haras. "This garden reminds me that things are not always easy. Even Jesus had difficult times, times when he had to set His mind to persevere."

Gradually his smile returned and began to fill his whole face. "God takes a risk in loving. Although He promised to be with us always, He doesn't hide or keep everything He treasures to Himself, like we often do. He loves His Son, yet He sent Him into the world knowing it was often a painful place. God is a keeper and a giver, a real paradox. He has a time when He builds and a time when He tears down. Sometimes He heals us instantly and we know He is the great healer, and sometimes we know without a doubt that our bodies are mortal and temporary. Sometimes in those places, it is even hard to pray. All we can do is trust and remind ourselves that He is love and He loves us."

Renner was silent for a moment and returned to that faraway place beyond her. Haras waited, wanting him to speak.

"Some things, like the granite in the ruins, last a long time. It's ancient, but we aren't." He took some snips from the pocket of his black gardening apron that hung about his hips, and cut a rose. "Some people only live on earth as long as a flower."

"They're so lovely," Haras said. "I love the red frill on the petals."

"Megagem loves the red frill too. I planted them for her." He handed the flower to Haras and she smelt its fragrance.

"They remind me of my mother."

Renner's eyes were moist. "We should enjoy people while they're with us, and remember the blessing of them from time to time, when they're gone." He touched one of the thorns on the rose. "Some things here on earth are hard and painful, like the thorns on the rose. Sometimes loving hurts. We are not in heaven yet."

Haras sighed.

Renner looked into her eyes and the sun seemed to be shining from within his face. "We do get a bit of a taste of heaven, though," he said.

Haras found herself smiling with him. Surely, this was what a real father was like. If she hadn't been hurt, would she ever have known? Suddenly the hurt seem less bothersome.

With the rose close to her nose, Haras inhaled deeply. She hoped she would find the photo again. She wanted to keep that, but she didn't want to hide it, like the button in her money bag. She wanted it displayed so she could enjoy it.

They walked towards the veranda together. Renner promised to make some enquires about her lost photo. He turned his nose up and sniffed. "What is that smell?"

Haras saw his alarm but couldn't smell anything. Ignoring the pain in her back, she rushed as fast as she could, towards the kitchen and Renner followed her.

"My dinner!"

Quail was her contribution to the shared meal. She had been secretly pleased she'd been able to make an expensive contribution and hoped it wasn't burnt. She wanted to repay Renner and Megagem for some of what they had done for her. She grabbed the oven mitt and opened the oven door.

Haras sighed with relief. "It's okay!" It's just a small chip from last night's meal, burnt to a crisp." She removed it from the oven.

"What are you cooking?" Renner asked.

Haras grinned. "You'll have to wait and see."

Chapter 26

Renner and Megagem often invited friends over for a shared meal. Everyone brought something different to eat. It was one of many things they did to *open up* their home. They said, heaven was open above for them and so their home was open down here for others too. It was an interesting concept and intrigued Haras.

She watched them - Hannah, Maham, and Eve, Bob, Nayan and Nosson - and stored up the memories. Their way of life was so different from hers. What they did, she decided she would do too.

She studied the guests when they arrived and noticed the ladies weren't wearing makeup, so she decided she wouldn't wear any either. She noticed they prayed before their meal, and sometimes afterwards too, all together. She made a mental note to make this her way of life as well. She hoarded all the doing things. Sometimes she would repeat their prayers thinking that, too, was what she should pray.

During one meal the conversation turned to ancient ruins and Haras's ears pricked up.

"What seems to be the quickest route is not always the quickest," Hannah said.

"No!" Eve chuckled. "Sometimes the quickest route is the long way round."

Haras remembered her first meeting with Renner. He'd appeared suddenly, out of nowhere, so she asked him, "How did you find me so quickly on the way to the ruins?"

"Ah!" Nosson answered for him. "He knows those rocks like his own back yard, and he is still nearly as surefooted as those goats he used to herd."

They all laughed. "He knows the hidden paths and streams around this land of ours."

The others nodded as though sharing some deep secret.

Haras was curious. She looked around at everyone. Were they talking figuratively or literally? "Do you all own the land?"

Hannah answered. "Some of it. Originally it all belonged to Renner's family, but after the earthquake, he gave some of it, including the ruins, to the town. Now we all own it, but we don't all know it like Renner does."

"It's too sad a subject for most to even talk about," Maham added.

Haras listened wide-eyed. She thought about the watering can and the flower-pot. They were broken things. Perhaps the people had hearts as sad as the stone-man, as broken as the ruins - as broken as the flower-pot. No wonder the garden was overgrown, a gift that no-one could bring themselves to take care of. Still, Haras was awed, as she thought about the gift. Fancy giving away something as valuable as the ruins!

"A tiny gift compared to all that Jesus has given me," Renner said, and Haras though he'd read her mind.

There was a pause in the conversation as everyone nodded. Haras looked around the table again, wondering why they were all so quiet. She waited for someone to say more, but only the sound of the clock ticking disturbed the deep silence. No-one elaborated and Haras leaned forward, waiting.

Bob broke the silence. "So, Renner, you said the stream is flowing again?"

"A little, just a little," he replied. "I saw it while searching for Haras."

Haras lost track of the conversation as she thought about this. She found herself listening again when she heard Renner say something about camping.

"We can make our camp around life's hard knocks and let them weigh us down, or we can let our heavenly Father take the weight of them from us."

Everyone was silent again.

Had they all lost someone they loved in the earthquake? Haras didn't like to ask. The white cross may have been a memorial for their children.

"… and not only hard knocks," Renner was saying. "Camping too long in one spot tends to get in the way of seeking and finding. Sometimes our camping can even replace the need for conversation with our heavenly Father."

Haras was back in the conversation. Bob picked up the theme. "Sometimes we camp too long around our preferred ways of doing things …"

"And words too," Nayan added. "We have a tendency to build traditions. Some are good, but sometimes they can become a bind."

"Like our possessions." Bob nodded.

"Like that rope Krad used to sell to the gold-seekers." Nosson said. "It bound him to the wrong path."

"The left path?" Haras added remembering what Renner had said about the right path being the right one.

Renner understood her and started to laugh then stopped. He drew in a deep breath.

Megagem looked at Renner then directed her question to the others. "Wasn't the rope business his son's?"

"Ah, that's right. The shop belonged to Ramar Krad, the ropes to Ara," Nosson said.

"Who are Ramar Krad and Ara?" Haras asked.

Renner turned to Haras and spoke quietly. "Ramar Krad used to own Klat's Store. His son Ara worked for him selling his ropes. He's the father of the young man who helped get you out of the ruins."

"You mean Nen?"

"That's him," Renner said.

"He visited me in hospital," Haras said.

Renner smiled. "Did he indeed?"

"He said he wanted to make sure I was okay." Haras fiddled with her napkin.

"Lovely boy," Megagem said. She exchanged looks with Hannah and they both smiled and nodded.

Eve looked at Haras. "Ramar tried to get rich quick at other people's expense." She pressed her lips tightly together, but not for long. "He ended up camping - no, more like being entombed - in the very land he helped to develop, the land of hard knocks."

They were back in their figurative language and Haras didn't know what they were talking about. "What did he do?"

"He's a con man. He conned people into buying prospecting rights that weren't his to sell and went to prison for it." The anger in Eve's voice startled Haras. Everyone stared at Eve and she lowered her head.

"He's back in town isn't he?" Bob's tone was kind.

Nayan nodded. "Yep, sure is. Saw him in a 4WD parked near the council building. His grandson's I suppose."

A few nodded and Eve kept on nodding as she slowly re-folded her napkin. "That grandson of his sure is good to him."

Megagem noded. "He's a Christian ..."

Maham patted her stomach. "Lovely meal, Haras."

"Too many meals like this and I'll have to start an exercise program," Nosson said, also patting his stomach.

Everyone laughed as they too patted theirs.

"Thank you, Haras," Nosson said. "You can come and cook for me any time you want."

"... and me," the others chimed in.

Megagem patted Renner on the arm. "We should pray for Ramar Krad before everyone leaves."

Everyone agreed and Eve prayed especially kindly for him. She said she hadn't realized she was still angry with him. She asked God to help her love him, as God loved her.

Haras felt grieved but didn't know why.

Chapter 27

Something red in the sky caught Haras's attention as she sat in the veranda shade the following afternoon. It was a hot air balloon. She stood and leaned over the metal rail hoping. She was waiting for Megagem and Renner to get back from Klat's, hoping they'd return with information, something she didn't already know. She watched the balloon until it became a small red lollipop on a single white cloud.

Everything about believing in God was so new to her. Nothing felt traditional. She wanted to be like her new friends. She wasn't sure which of the things they said and did would be considered *camping too long in one spot* if she did them too.

The idea of building tombs around life's *hard knocks* was more familiar to her. She knew she did that. She'd spent her life replaying imaginary conversations with her imaginary father. Sometimes she'd liked the feeling of sadness and self-pity, and encouraged them. Sometimes she'd wanted others to feel sad for her as well, because they had a father and she didn't. She had played on this for her own advantage more than once, especially at school, if she thought her teacher was soft-hearted.

Haras went back to her chair. She closed the Bible and took it back inside to her bedroom. She'd been reading a parable about a man who knew God's kingdom was worth everything he had. She looked at the reflection of the urn in the mirror.

Mirror, mirror on the wall, what is the greatest treasure of them all?

The thought surprised her. The answer was easy. Of course the *right* answer was her Heavenly Father, but what did that look like? Was God always like treasure hidden in a field? Was He always someone so valuable, He was worth everything she owned in order to keep?

Haras decided He was, but saying so was easy. Putting it into practice sounded scary. She knew some people who'd been Christians most of their life, yet they seemed to be hanging onto all sorts of things, as though their lives depended on them. Didn't they see how valuable God was? Renner and Megagem did. She hoped she would learn to value God like them.

The sound of singing interrupted her thoughts. She caught a glimpse of Megagem outside her window. At last they were back from their shopping trip. She raced to open the front door. "That didn't take long, or is my watch slow? Where's Renner? Did he learn anything?"

"He's coming, so don't panic. How about a pot of tea?"

"Okay. Here, let me take the groceries. You go and sit down. I'll bring the tea into the lounge."

"Thanks, Haras. I was hoping you'd say that."

Renner came into the kitchen with a chocolate cake. "Is it tea in the lounge with chocolate cake?"

Haras laughed. "And everything you have to tell me. I'm trying to hold my tongue and not rush you."

Renner laughed too. "I see. I see. I'll move as fast as I can."

He put the cake on a plate and followed Haras into the lounge. "Well," he said as he leaned back into the couch and clasped his hands behind his head. "Well, we went to Klat's and people were chatting, like they normally do. Then I saw Ramar Krad. That was a surprise. He wasn't chatting though. No surprise there."

"Nen's grandfather?" Haras pictured his dark curly hair, remembered his aftershave —.

Renner cut a slice of cake and continued. "Ramar Krad was sitting by himself. He looked pretty angry."

"That made me feel sad," Megagem said.

Renner tilted his head, and Haras was touched at the tender way he looked at Megagem.

"Yes," Renner said. "Ramar Krad's been told he isn't welcome in the store, or anywhere in town for that matter, yet he braves everyone's scowls and scowls himself."

Haras put her cup down. "Why?"

"He was a con man. Went to prison. People don't trust him."

"It must be so hard for him coming into the store." Megagem said. "I tried to make him feel welcome without offending the others." She turned to Haras. "I asked around about the missing photo. I could see Ramar Krad listening intently, so I asked him, too. No-one had seen the photo lying around."

"Ramar told me he'd never even heard about a girl called Haras, let alone seen her photo. He said Deerg was a common name. It is. He called out to a man called Deerg, who was sitting by the window … asked him if he had a daughter. That nearly caused a riot. The man called Deerg wasn't pleased."

Haras leaned towards Megagem. "A man called Deerg?"

Renner motioned for her to sit back again. "Don't get excited Haras."

"Deerg said he's never been out of the country, and the only child he had died in the ruins," Megagem said.

"His surname wasn't Anona," Renner added.

Haras was disappointed. "Oh." She'd already told them her grandparents had rented a place in Y'kahs and her father had gone looking for gold. Renner had said a few Deerg's had tried their hand, prospecting on his land. She recalled his words.

"Can't remember their surnames. Sorry. A few came from as far away as Australia. Ramar Krad advertised the gold prospecting opportunity there. I suppose he reckoned Australia was far enough away to discourage people from checking the place out before buying the prospecting rights he was selling," Renner had rubbed his brow. "They didn't make their fortune, though. Maybe one of them was your father."

"Where did they go?" Haras had asked.

"Probably back home."

Haras sat back, assailed by doubt. It was just impossible. She had no new leads to follow. Her father might not even be alive. Everyone else had died.

Chapter 11

"Now here comes the local news, courtesy of Radio Gos." A girl about her own age was calling out as she cupped a rolled up pew sheet like a microphone. This was Haras's first visit to Renner and Megagem's church and the introduction startled her. She turned to see who *Radio Gos* was. None of the girls in the group appeared to be offended, and nor did *Radio Gos*.

Assa, whom Haras had met before the church service, introduced her. "Haras, meet Gos. It's short for *it's the gospel truth* which used to be her favourite saying."

"... and *gossip*," another girl added and giggled. Gos pulled a face at the *gossip* commenter and curtseyed at Haras.

"A new princess in the Kingdom. Pleased to meet you. Megagem told me to look out for you." She curled a wisp of her short dark hair around her finger and let it go.

Taken aback, Haras realized her mouth was still open and closed it. "Gos?" she asked.

"Yeah I guess it's short for gossip, but I like to think of it as getting to know everyone." She beamed around at everyone. "I can't help it if I see and hear everything that's going on around here. There's so little of it, and how else are you all going to catch up on what's been happening?" She laughed, and then looked straight at Haras. "No, it's really short for gosling." She held her arms out like wings. "I'm about to change into a swan." She did a little dance and they all laughed.

"Well, Swanny, what's the goss?" The girl who'd called her *gossip* linked her arm through hers. They were obviously good enough friends to give and take the banter.

Haras relaxed a bit.

"So, you're the girl who was rescued by the gorgeous Nen? I wish it had been me in his arms being rescued." Gos flapped her wings again. "I wouldn't mind getting lost if he came to find me."

"Gos!" Hannah said.

Gos smacked her own hand. "Duly disciplined … but did you know Nen's back in town?"

"No. How do you know?" Assa asked.

Gos placed her hands around an imaginary microphone.

"Tune in to Radio Gos!" She motioned for everyone to come closer.

"We're all ears," Assa said and they all giggled again.

"He brought his grandfather for a visit and I saw them both go into Klat's store," Gos said. "I was in the car giving my nails a makeover, waiting for my father." She wiggled her nails for everyone to see and twirled her bracelet so everyone could see the colour match. "New, a pressie from Mum. That's how come I saw Nen." She batted her long dark lashes.

"Did you go into the store?" Hannah asked.

"What, and let him think I was chasing him? Not likely."

The girls giggled. Haras was all ears.

"Anyway I couldn't. My nails were wet."

Everyone laughed again, then feigned disappointment.

"Oh dear!"

"Too bad."

"How frustrating."

"Wet nails are so like that!"

Assa tilted her head and addressed Haras. "Nen found you at the ruins?"

Everyone turned their attention to Haras. Some said they'd read about the accident in the local paper; others said they'd heard it on the news.

"I saw the newspaper report too," Haras said. "I sent it to a friend."

They all wanted to know more about the accident and plied her with questions. They wanted to know more about her and Nen too, so she filled them in on her rescue story. She didn't know anything about Nen. She wished they'd kept talking about him, but she didn't ply them with questions. She didn't want to appear to be seeking gossip, seeing that some of them seemed to be smitten by him.

"So you cried out to Jesus and He sent Nen to save you. Wow, what a testimony!"

"And Renner," Haras said.

"And helicopter medics," Gos said.

"I had my eyes closed most of the time, so I didn't really see my rescuers."

"Closed? Were you praying?" Hannah asked.

"No. The light was too bright and my body hurt too much."

"Oh." The girls abandoned their banter and became genuinely concerned. "Are you still in pain?"

"No, but I still can't bend over, can't do my own boots up. I'm having physiotherapy now the bruises have faded."

A few boys wandered over and Hannah introduced them. It was their mid-term break and some were spending it at home with their parents, so they had lots to catch up on.

The group soon began to break up and Hannah asked Haras if she'd like to join her and Gos for a movie sometime. They didn't go to uni, so wouldn't be rushing off again in a few days like some of the others.

"We hardly ever go." Hannah said. "Nothing much on, but when there is, we do. And there's a good one showing in a couple of weeks."

"I'd love to. I don't have transport though, and I can't walk very far yet."

"No problem. I'll pick you up. I can drop you and Gos right at the theatre door and then park the car," Hannah said.

"Where is the theatre? I haven't seen any around here."

"No, our town's too small for one. We drive into the city, make a day of it. Sometimes we shop till we drop then take in the movie, but we won't if you can't walk much." Hannah tilted her head and Haras caught her look of genuine concern.

"Sometimes we take a picnic basket and stop half-way."

"Sounds like fun," Haras said.

Hannah laughed. "And sometimes we take the boys too."

"More fun!" Gos rolled her eyes and she nodded.

"But not in one car, of course."

Gos nodded again. "Of course. Gotta go. See ya next time." She waved and headed back towards the church.

"We try to abide by the laws of the land," Hannah said. "One seat belt per person." She laughed and Haras grinned. She was beginning to like Hannah.

Megagem joined them. "I'm glad to see you're making friends, Haras. I've known Hannah all her life." Megagem reached out to ruffle Hannah's red dyed curls. She pulled away in time.

"Aw, Meg."

"I know. You're not a kid any more. It's just that your hair …"

"… is so lovely. Yeah, yeah I know. Every week I know!"

Renner joined them. "You know?"

"Yes I know!" Hannah pointed to her red hair. Renner smiled. He shook his keys. "Are you ready to go Haras, Megagem?"

They nodded.

Hannah took her own keys from her bag. "Glad you came, Haras. If you're here next week, I'll give you the details of our movie trip. Okay?"

"Thank's Hannah. I'd like that. Bye." Haras followed Renner to the car and waved through the window.

On the way home Haras thought about Nen. All the talk about him made her curious. She pulled out her phone and searched his name online. It was Egyptian. It meant ancient waters. That sounded exotic.

Ancient waters and an ancient path. She smiled as she formed the link between his name and her urn, then frowned. She wished her own name meant something exotic.

Haras found Nen's social network page. He was an environmental engineer. She didn't know what that was, so she searched that too. Megagem turned and asked her if she'd found anything interesting.

Haras put her phone away and changed the subject. "Would you like me to make a vegetarian casserole for dinner?"

Megagem chuckled and nodded.

Chapter

Over me, all around,
Even in my heart,
Your love is like the gentle rain,
Healing all my pain.

Hannah, Gos and Assa sang softly, repeating the chorus so Haras could learn the words. Their music filled the car with a tangible presence of peace. Haras leaned back and drank it in as she studied Assa's newly streaked hair. How different the three girls were. They had even chosen different hair colours. Gos had dyed hers black, Hannah's was red, and Assa's looked amazing with blue and purple streaks. Haras was glad she was back to her natural dark brown. Her red had finally grown out.

"We're half way there," Hannah said and pointed to a side road. Almost immediately, the car began making a thud thud sound.

"Oh no!" Hannah wailed. She slowed down.

"Flat tyre?" Haras asked.

"Feels like it. Car's pulling to the right. She stopped and got out to check. "Yep. It's flat. Oh blow!" There wasn't another car in sight.

The others got out and stood looking at it.

Hannah slapped both hands on her hips. "I've never had to change a tyre before. I've seen it done, but never had to do it myself."

"Well, I've done it once," Haras said. "But I can't bend down to do it now."

"Why don't we have lunch?" Assa said. "Someone might drive past and take pity on us." Gos agreed. Hannah prayed aloud, asking God for help. Gos opened the boot and reached in for the food hamper.

"Between us we can do it," Haras assured Hannah. "I can tell you what to do, and you can do it."

Assa pulled a ground sheet out and began looking for a place to sit.

Gos pointed to an odd shaped tree. Half of its trunk swung down then up like a swing. The other reached straight and high.

"By that Pine tree, Assa. It's close enough to watch out for cars coming and far enough away not to be covered in dust if one does."

They all agreed and headed for it.

"God can work all things for our good," Assa said. "Even this flat tyre." She prayed aloud that He would. "Last year I dropped my necklace behind the washing machine. I had to take the hose out of the outlet hole before I could move the machine to get my necklace. I forgot to put the hose back in because my phone rang, and the next time I did the washing, the water flooded the floor. Mum came home and told me it wasn't the best way to wash the floor."

Everyone laughed.

"But she said she was pleased that I was doing it because the floor needed washing, and she was worn out!"

Hannah handed Assa a sandwich.

"Thanks Hannah. Thanks Jesus."

"Amen," Hannah said.

Gos pointed to the car. "So what good do you think will come of this?"

They all munched in silence. Hannah poured drinks for everyone and encouraged everyone to help herself to the rest of the food. They did.

"There's someone!" Haras pointed past the car. "Someone coming down that side road we passed."

They all turned to where she was pointing.

"He's got a backpack."

Hannah pulled a face. "A hitchhiker?"

Gos was on her feet. "Not likely on this stretch of road. Who would try hitchhiking on this road?"

They started packing the hamper as the man approached the car.

"Do you think he's safe?" Hannah asked.

"Well, there are four of us." Gos said striding out towards the car. The others followed with the picnic gear. "And he doesn't look like a strongman, more like a uni student."

The man stopped and looked at the tyre. He scratched his very short trimmed, black beard, and waved at the girls. "I see you've got a flat tyre."

"Yep." Hannah frowned.

"Need help changing it?"

Hannah nodded. "Yes, please. That would be amazing!"

He smiled, took his backpack off and asked for the jack and spare tyre. Hannah opened the boot for him.

"Thank you so much. I've never had to change one."

"My pleasure. I've never had to hitchhike before."

"So you *are* hitchhiking?" Gos asked. "I would've thought it a bit dangerous. This road isn't known for its traffic and no-one stops to pick hitchhikers up anymore. We wouldn't have."

"No, I know. My parents live not far from here. I made a flying visit for Mum's birthday. I missed the bus back and have to get back to uni today." He pushed the jack under the car and began cranking. The car rose and he loosened the lug nuts. He looked back at the girls as they stood watching.

"I'm Reinier, by the way."

"What are you studying at uni?" Haras asked.

"Counselling."

Gos leaned forward. "Not car mechanics?"

They all laughed.

"No. Anything's possible though. Never know when you might need a skill like that."

"Indeed." Gos said and looked at her nails.

Reinier noticed. "Not your cup of tea I suppose?" He raised an eyebrow and Gos shook her head. "Spoil my nails!"

He chuckled and soon had the spare tyre on. "There." He handed Hannah the wrench. "That should get you to the city, but I'd have the nuts tightened when you replace the flat tyre if I were you."

Hannah thanked him as he lifted the flat tyre and put it in the boot. Assa gave the jack to Hannah and she put it away as Reinier put his back pack on and held up his thumb at the empty road.

"Would you like a lift?" Hannah asked.

"Thought you'd never ask." Reinier beamed. "You are an answer to prayer."

"Really?" Assa opened her eyes wide. "Well, you're an answer to Hannah's prayer too!"

"Really?" He looked at them, amazement written all over his face.

Hannah closed the boot. "Are you a Christian?"

Reiner slipped his backpack off again. "Yes, are you?"

"We all are," Assa said.

"Well. That's just too amazing.

Hannah introduced them all and offered him the front seat next to her. She thought his long legs might be squashed in the back seat. Haras thought there were other reasons too. They were confirmed as she listened to their animated conversation the rest of the way. They hardly noticed the others in the car and they exchanged contact details before he was dropped off.

"What good can ever come of a flat tyre?" Assa teased Hannah as they continued on to the movie theatre.

Hannah looked at her watch and grinned. "Anything's possible on this journey, even being on time for the movie!"

Chapter **11**

Pictures of the earthquake flashed into Haras's mind as she sat on her bed. Her mind was right back there at the ruins, reliving the pain, adding it to her list of reasons to be sad. She eased herself up from her bed and tried to bend over. No. She still couldn't do it comfortably. The sound of Megagem's singing floated through the bedroom wall.

"I am the Lord that healeth thee ..."

Why didn't Jesus just heal her? She believed He could and she had prayed. The girls had prayed for her too, on the way home from the movie, but nothing had happened. She looked at her watch. Too early to phone Ahsha. She reached for her Bible and flicked through the pages.

You have shaken the earth. You have split it.

The words leapt out from a page. They spoke to her very situation. She continued reading.

... heal its fractures for it is slipping.

"Yes," her heart cried.

... But for those who fear you, you have given a banner so they can escape before the bow.

She pictured a banner blowing in the wind with Jesus as a lion; a symbol of authority. The sight of the banner would strike fear in the enemy archers. She wanted that banner! Instead, *she* was the broken flower-pot and the broken watering can! She was *quaking* and not only *quaking* and slipping, she was weary from all the hard knocks in her life. There was no good in still being broken.

A banner has been given.

Haras stopped her self-talk. She'd been about to relive all her *hard knocks* again, adding one on top of the other. Did she have to stop doing that? Were those thoughts like the archer's arrows? Didn't she just have to pray and believe, and Jesus would do the rest? She rubbed her temple.

Haras determined to pray, instead of reliving her pain. Maybe that would unfurl the banner. The prayer of the Psalmist would be her prayer. She would *camp* around it until God answered her. She re-read Psalm 60 and pleaded again with her heavenly Father.

"Please mend my fractures. Take the weight of my hard knocks and heal me." She didn't notice anything change. She began to think about the banner and the authority it represented, and then something *did* happen. It felt like sunlight dispelling a dark blanket of discouragement and self-pity.

Haras looked at her watch again. It was nearly Ahsha's lunch break. She had so much to tell her. It was hard waiting.

Finally! Haras picked up her phone and made the call. Ahsha answered and Haras told her all about the movie trip, the flat tyre and how it all worked out. By the time she'd finished telling her all about it, every bit of discouragement had fled.

"Wow. God let that happen, a flat tyre at just the right time and place, so a hitchhiker would get a ride? Maybe He did it so He could introduce two people to each other. Wow!"

Haras told her about Assa's flooded laundry floor and how it needed cleaning.

"God does do miracles, doesn't He?"

"Well, I wouldn't call that a miracle," Ahsha said. "A nudge in the right direction maybe?"

They laughed.

"I haven't experienced any miracles, but I know God does them. The Bible's full of them," Ahsha said.

Haras agreed, although she had experienced God's help in hospital.

"I want a miracle healing right now," Haras said. She lay back on her bed and kicked her slippers off. "I want to go walking and I want to be able to bend down and tie my boot laces."

"Mmm. I guess a lot of people want instant healing," Ahsha said. "But we still have a mortal body. We have the ability to feel pain, so I guess we do have to put up with it from time to time."

"Well, I think I will pursue healing. The Samaritan woman pursued Jesus and He gave her what she wanted."

Ahsha was quiet.

"Are you still there?"

"Yes."

"Anyway enough about me. What's happening your end?" Haras heard Ahsha take a deep breath.

"You know that new doctor?"

Haras giggled. "He asked you out?"

"Yep."

"Okay, what's he like?"

"Nice enough, I suppose, but he's not a Christian. I said yes, but now I regret it. I don't think I should go out with him."

"Do you think he's really keen?"

"Don't know, maybe a bit lonely."

"Well, ask him to church."

"Hmm."

Ahsha changed the subject and began to fill Haras in on what she'd been doing. She was saving hard for a holiday.

"I might even come visit you," she said, and Haras heard her swallow her drink. "Oops, drank that too fast."

Haras wriggled her toes. "You'd really come over? That would be some holiday!"

"I'm thinking about it."

"It would be great to see you. We could go out to the ruins and explore."

"Don't get too excited. You know I hate travelling. I don't know about going to the ruins either - sounds too dangerous to me. Anyway it will take some time to get enough saved to think seriously about it."

They continued chatting until Ahsha had to go.

Haras swung her legs back over the side of the bed and sat up. She began planning what the'd do if Ahsha did come. The seed was planted and it grew in Haras's mind, even though Ahsha hated travelling and hadn't made a decision.

Chapter Q

"Questions, so many questions! I'm like a little child going on a journey and replaying the same question over and over again: Are we there yet? When will God heal me?" Haras said.

Renner took his eyes from the road for a moment and Haras saw he was smiling at her.

"In His time. In His time." He turned his attention back to driving.

Replaying positive words was something Haras associated with Renner. It made her smile each time she caught him doing it and he did it each time he drove her to the hospital for physiotherapy. It had become a regular *outing* in Haras's life, and exercises a regular *innings* in her new home. Renner always commented about enjoying the *outing*, which always made her feel more comfortable about being given so much.

She wanted to give something back, but Renner, and Megagem too, would always say that she was enough of a gift for them. Once Renner had said, "Love cannot be earned or it isn't love," and once he'd even said, "We love you, little flower," just like Megagem sometimes did.

Haras knew she was like a flower to them and sometimes she felt like one too, a flower beginning to beam in their kindness, but not a *little* one. They had all laughed as she stood tall and patted Megagem on the head to emphasize how tall she was. She did like the image they planted in her mind though. The way of flowers was just to be. They didn't have to do anything. They were the reward for the gardener's work.

Renner dropped Haras off at the hospital and she found a seat in the waiting room. As she waited, Haras realised she hadn't even thought about finding her father for two whole weeks, maybe more.

The physiotherapist appeared with a wad of papers in his hand. He asked Haras if she minded having a student to work with her. Her name was Releah.

"Re - leah?" Haras frowned.

The physiotherapist clicked the end of his pen and waited for her reply. "Well?"

Questions arose in Haras's mind. Of course she didn't mind being attended to by a student physiotherapist, but where had she heard that name before?

Haras was sitting on the edge of the bed when the student came in. She immediately recognized her long black, plaited hair. She'd seen Releah at church. She'd come with a visiting preacher.

Releah didn't recognize Haras. Not until she told her where she'd seen her.

During the physio session, Releah checked Haras's mobility. When she said, "Bend over!" Haras found herself bending over, and at the same time, she saw light around the side of the broken rib. She immediately knew the light was Jesus. It was the first time since the accident she'd been able to bend right over.

When the physio session was finished, Haras told Renner and phoned Hannah.

"An amazing thing happened at physio today. I saw Jesus as light and now I can bend over."

"Wow, really? That's amazing. What did He look like?" Hannah asked.

"Light." Haras said.

Renner listened and they both beamed all the way home. Megagem hugged her close, then looked at her face and hugged her again. She was speechless and just beamed.

Haras couldn't wait to phone Ahsha. She was excited and restless. What a pain it had been, having to ask Megagem to do her boot-laces up for her. Now she was able to do them herself! When she finally got through to Ahsha, she talked non-stop retelling the amazing incident. She almost forgot to ask Ahsha about her doctor. Had she asked him to church? She had and he'd declined so that was that, as far as she was concerned. She was more interested in hearing about the light.

The following Sunday Haras couldn't help smiling as she walked to church. It felt so good to be able to walk a reasonable distance again, even though her muscles felt weak. She arrived early and a small group of adults invited her to join them in praying for the service.

While they were praying, Haras felt her whole body relax so much she thought she was going to slip off the chair and onto the floor. She held onto the sides of the chair and managed to stay seated. During the service, Haras turned her head. It no longer felt stiff. Every so often she tested it. It didn't hurt. She beamed through the rest of the service.

"You've been smiling all through church, and you still are. What's up?" Gos asked.

"Something strange happened to me while we were praying before the service," Haras said. She demonstrated her new mobility. "Now I can turn my head and it isn't stiff, and my body—." She wriggled. "It feels kinda loose. I think God must have answered my prayer! I think He's mended my body."

"God's so good. Wow. That's awesome!" Gos gave her a quick hug and was soon telling everyone about Haras's healing. Megagem put her hand in Renner's at the news and they exchanged glances. They looked as happy as Haras felt.

All the way home Haras silently thanked God for answering her prayer and she felt sure He would mend her heart too. There was already so much joy bubbling inside her.

Haras began building up her strength by gradually increasing the time she spent walking. The stronger she got, the more her mind wandered down the old worry paths. Was her father still alive? If he was, would he have another family? How would he react to her? If she ever did find Deerg, would he believe she was his daughter? She didn't even have the photo to convince him now. Would he even like her? What if …

Reviewing the lack of evidence for her father's identity put lead weights on her feet. She began dragging them around the house.

One day, she flopped onto the couch, held down by a blanket of dark thoughts. Where could her father be? Then she remembered the *banner*. Her heavenly Father would know where her earthly father was! She began praying for him and a trickle of hope penetrated the heavy blanket. Maybe one day she would get to meet him.

Haras stood, picked up the new drawing pad and pencil Megagem had bought her, and went outside to the courtyard. She twirled her pencil and stared at the blank art paper before her. A drawing a day would help improve her ability, Megagem had said, but what would she draw today? Her mind wandered. Renner had told her, no-one had seen her missing photo lying around. Deerg was a common name. Haras knew that. Renner's news or lack of it only added to her frustration. She wanted her missing photo.

"Don't go to pieces about anything; instead exchange wishes. Petition, and make requests to God about everything with gratitude."

The words she'd read from her Bible that morning hit her sore spot and so she prayed again about her photo. She told God what she wished for, even though she had done so a million times, well, it felt like that many. Haras put her pencil down. *"everything with gratitude."* She hadn't done that a million times. She began by thanking God for Renner and Megagem, then for every other thing she could think of. It cheered her up and made her feel less lethargic. She opened her free hand and began sketching it.

Chapter 

Rust. How do I draw rust? Haras flipped through her art pad, pleased she could see some improvement in her daily sketches, and found a clean page. She would need another art pad soon. She put her pencil down and took a sip of cold fruit drink, while she studied the rust on the veranda handrail. Movement near the gate caught her eye. A man had stopped there, and she was the only person home that day. Whatever the man wanted, he was out of luck. Probably a salesman, judging by the suit he was wearing. Black curly hair—It was Nen! He had trimmed his hair. He waved at her.

Haras pressed her lips together. He was too friendly—too attractive. His whole body smiled.

"Hi, you look a lot better than the last time I saw you."

"Hello …" She forced her eyes from his dark curly hair, tanned face and sparkling brown eyes. He was holding her missing things.

"My sleeping bag! My backpack! "You found them!" She opened the gate and invited him in.

He held out his free hand. Haras shook it and stared.

"I visited you in hospital."

A touch of colour flushed his cheeks. He lowered his eyes and handed her the sleeping bag.

"Yes, I do remember. Thanks again for the flowers. The newspaper report mentioned you. The hospital nurses told me you helped me too." He'd already told her that in hospital. She was talking too quickly.

"Yep."

"Thanks."

"My grandfather was talking with Renner some time ago …"

"Ramar Krad?" Haras blurted out.

His eyes opened wide and he stared long and hard at her before replying. "Yes." He stepped back and frowned. "Do you know my grandfather?"

Haras wished she hadn't opened her mouth. "No. I heard Renner telling Megagem that Ramar Krad was back in town, and that his grandson brought him for a visit. He mentioned your name and I put two and two together." She didn't tell him she'd also been listening to gossip about the family, or about how some of the girls at church had mentioned Ramar Krad's good-looking grandson. Nor did she tell him that she'd checked him out on a few social networks.

"My grandfather told me you lost some of your things at the ruins. I had some work to do out that way myself, so I did a good search for them. I found them, probably where you left them - a dry spot on a ledge. Right where I usually make my camp bed."

Haras blinked and stared at him. "Your bed? Do you go out there a lot?"

"From time to time. I keep an eye on the place. Mostly safety reasons. Do some contract work for the local council. They don't encourage tourists to visit the ruins, but it still needs to be safe." He ran a finger around his collar as though he wanted to undo his top button, but didn't.

Haras liked his lean look, but he did look hot in his suit. She felt nervous and pointed to the courtyard chairs. "Do you have time for a cold drink?"

"Thank you. I do," he smiled, and followed her to the chairs, where he placed her gear.

"I'll get the juice. Orange okay for you?"

It was.

Haras and Nen sipped quietly and it felt like an age of silence to Haras. She was glad when he broke the silence by pulling an envelope from his pocket.

"I went through the bag, looking for some identification to make sure it was yours. I hope you don't mind." He handed her the envelope. "The lady looks like you."

It was her photo! He'd found her photo. "Thank you! I've been looking everywhere for this. Thank you."

Nen grinned as he nodded.

Haras nodded too. "She's my grandmother." She pointed to the young man in the photo. "And he's my father, although I've never met him."

Nen lowered his voice. "My father did." He was no longer smiling.

Haras's breathing quickened. "Your father? Please tell me what you know about him. Deerg left my mother before I was born. He doesn't even know I exist. How did your father meet him? Where?"

Nen pressed his lips together and looked at his hands, spread wide on the table. "Well, you're bound to find out sooner or later, so I might as well tell you."

Haras looked at his hands too. They didn't look like Renner's gardening hands. They looked neat and clean, like the rest of him. She took a quick look at her own and was glad she hadn't been in the garden.

"My grandfather came up with a 'get rich quick' scheme. He called it an opportunity of a lifetime, a 's-e-h-c-i-r journey,'" he said.

Haras gasped. "My mother told me that."

Nen smiled sadly. "The Seh-cir journey was really a gold rush. The man in the photo, Deerg, was one of many gold seekers. My grandfather sold him a package deal that included the rights to mine a small area of land by the ancient ruins. It backed onto the stream, but it was a hard place to get to in those days. Do you remember Klat's store?"

Haras looked down at her hands again and took a sip of her drink. "Yes. Megagem loves their chocolate cakes."

"Well, it used to belong to my grandfather, only he didn't sell the range of things they sell now—no food or other general store stuff." He smiled. "My father worked for him building up his own range of ropes, and my grandfather helped him through illegal means." He frowned and ran his fingers through the back of his dark curly hair. "The land wasn't my grandfather's to sell. Your father was among those who took him to court, when they found they didn't own the rights to mine the land. My grandfather paid for his fraud in prison. He lost his business too, which made him a very angry and bitter man." Nen took a sip from his drink and looked at his watch.

Haras leaned forward wanting to hear more. "Fraud?"

"I don't know if my father knew what his father was up to at the time, but they both lost more than what my grandfather stole." Nen looked at Haras. His jaw set hard. "The reason I'm telling you all this is ..." He looked down at his drink again before continuing. "He knows you are Deerg's daughter. He saw the photo and is still very angry with your father ... and the others who took him to court. Sometimes my aunt stirs him up too. My grandfather swore he would get back what belonged to him. He hasn't, though." Nen ran his hand through his hair. "I think he's hatching another mad plan. If we get a whiff of it, my father and I will steer him away from it."

Haras looked at the photo again. "Court? Fraud?" She couldn't take it all in. Her father conned by Nen's grandfather? Had she left the photo on the ledge with the other things? She couldn't remember doing that. Nen's grandfather a con man?

Nen interrupted her racing, jumbled thoughts. "Perhaps Deerg left as soon as the court case finished, along with the others. I suppose they all went back to the four corners of the earth. I wouldn't have hung around if I'd been any one of them."

Haras was disappointed. "I was hoping to find my father here in Y'kahs, not some other corner of the earth."

"Have you contacted Interpol?"

"Who?"

"Interpol."

"I've never heard of them."

"They are pretty good at finding people I believe."

Haras relaxed back in her chair. *Interpol.* She reminded herself that nothing was impossible with God. Those were the very words they'd sung in church that week, and here was another avenue she could try.

"Stay away from my grandfather," Nen warned. He may be old but he is still capable of taking revenge."

Haras gripped the chair as anxiety squashed the glimmer of hope. Nen lowered his eyes but not before Haras caught a flicker of sorrow in their darkness. She relaxed her grip on the chair.

"Even a small pebble makes a ripple in the water." Nen said. "My father lost a lot of friends. Some believed he was involved in the fraud, but he was a young man, pretty gullible in those days. Some still say I'm tarred with the same brush. Like father, like son. And like grandson ... but I'm neither like my father nor my grandfather. Sometimes I feel like going to some other corner of the world myself, but my family's here, and I need to keep them on the straight and narrow. Well, sort of!"

Haras thought she saw the beginning of a grin. "Do *you* keep to the straight and narrow then?" her hand flew to her mouth. Where had that come from? She hadn't meant to be that forward.

He looked at her and gave a half laugh that made Haras's stomach quiver.

"Did the earthquake change the ruins?" she asked.

"The earthquake toppled a few rocks. It allowed the stream to flow above ground again too."

Haras was intrigued. Having followed the streambed, she wondered if it was flowing over it or in a new direction.

Nen answered her thoughts. "As far as I could see, it's flowing over the old bed, but I couldn't be sure. I didn't follow it." He turned as the automatic double gate opened, and a car drove in.

Haras stood. "Megagem and Renner are back. They might need a hand with the groceries."

Nen swallowed the last mouthful of his drink and Haras did too.

"I'll just go and see," she said.

Nen followed her to the garage. Haras saw the surprise on their faces as he greeted them and offered to carry some of their bags.

"Nice to see you, Nen. What brings you here?"

Nen glanced towards Haras. "Haras. I found her things at the ruins."

"Oh, that's great news." Renner's face wrinkled with smiles. "Well, well, Haras. No wonder you are all smiles." He chuckled as he handed Nen a bag.

Haras took the last bag and followed Megagem, who kept repeating, "Thank you Jesus."

By the time they reached the kitchen, Haras was also praising God with silent thank you's.

Renner pointed to the kitchen bench. "Thanks, Nen. Here will be fine." He pulled out a chair and sat down, flopping his hands on his knees. "Ah! That's a good job done. I'm ready for lunch!" He looked up at Nen. "Would you like to stay for lunch?"

Nen looked at his watch and frowned. Megagem pressed him to stay.

"I'll see if I can reschedule an appointment," he said and left the room, taping on his phone. He was smiling when he returned. "Yes, I'd love to stay. Thanks"

Haras looked away. She'd been staring and didn't want him to see how pleased she was.

"Salad and pizza. Thank you Jesus!" Triumph was written all over Megagem's face as she produced a fast-food lunch from the top of one of the grocery bags.

"Yes, thank you Jesus!" Renner echoed.

"Amen." Nen said and Haras voiced her thanks without thinking as she stared wide-eyed at Nen.

"So you *are* a Christian then?" she said.

"I am." Nen looked at Haras. "Are you?"

"Yes, a new one."

Renner took a slice of pizza and looked at Nen. "So Nen, you found Haras's camping gear?"

Nen nodded and told them how he'd searched for it when he was out at the ruins assessing the damage from the earthquake.

Renner frowned. "Is anything going to be done to make the place safer and more accessible?"

"I'm looking into it. Takes an accident to get things moving."

"Hmm." Renner took another bite of his pizza and chewed it slowly.

"Thanks. I enjoyed that," Nen said as he finished the last piece.

"Me too," Haras said.

Renner leaned back in his chair when he'd finished and folded his arms. "Good company and good food!"

Megagem stood to clear the table. "I thought you called it junk food." There was a gleam of triumph in her eyes again.

"Ah well, you proved me wrong again. Just as well you got your way. Three pies would not have been as easy to share as pizza."

Haras enjoyed listening to their gentle banter. It made her feel safe. She got up to help clear the table. Nen moved to help as well, but Renner insisted he sit down again. He did.

"So Nen, are you living at home again?"

"No, although my mother sometimes thinks I do … when she sees all the washing I bring." He fiddled with his napkin. "I'm working in the area and brought my grandfather for a visit. He's staying for a while as he doesn't drive anymore. He doesn't usually feel inclined to stay, but this time he does." He looked at his watch and pushed his chair back. "Well, I must go. Thank you for the lunch."

His abruptness stopped the conversation, but not the question in Haras's mind. *Why was his grandfather inclined to stay?*

Renner stood and extended his hand. "Thank you for bringing Haras's things back."

Nen shook it and nodded at Megagem and Haras.

"No trouble." He looked at Haras. "I was out there a few days before the earthquake."

"The white cross? Did *you* weed around it?" Haras asked.

Nen looked at Haras briefly. "So you saw it?" He glanced at Megagem. Haras saw the laughter fade from his eyes.

"Yes. It gets pretty overgrown. I do it for a family friend, when I'm out there. You nearly knocked her over when you left Klat's store!"

Haras was speechless. So, he saw that too. "Did you hear what she said to me?"

"No. Did she warn you not to go to the ruins?"

"Yes."

"She warns every new face she sees, I guess, even if they have no intention of going out there. Just as well there aren't that many new faces. Two of her children died out there in an earthquake, so she gets a bit fierce about the place, but don't worry about her." Nen combed his hair with his fingers. "She looks kinda ancient and scary, but when you get to know her she's a rare gem … like Megagem here."

Megagem slapped her hands on her hips. "Ancient and scary? Is that what I look like?"

Nen flashed a smile at Megagem and headed towards the door. "No, I meant the *gem* bit." He paused and looked back at Haras. "I hope I see you again."

Haras snapped back from her encounter with the ancient woman. "I, I hope so too." Her mind continued working overtime, hatching an idea! She could see their friendship leading to a healing in Nen's grandfather; one that would help him give up his desire for revenge. It wasn't impossible and friendship with Nen … well!

Chapter

The sound of her mother's favourite expletive was on the tip of Haras's tongue. She resisted the urge to throw it into the wardrobe with her boots, and flopped onto her bed. She'd unsuccessfully tried to get information from the court, the police, and various travel agencies. Now she was hot and sticky, her socks wet. She pulled them off and threw them on the floor. Waiting for a reply from Interpol was hard. Waiting in queues was harder, especially when the waiting yielded nothing and it was hot. What was she to do?

Haras leaned back with her arms behind her head. Hannah had moved to the city to be near Reinier. They were talking about getting engaged. Assa and Gos were thinking about moving too. They complained there was even less to do in town now that Hannah had moved. Everyone had itchy feet—well apart from Renner and Megagem. And … she thought she'd seen Izzi getting into a red car in the city. She'd waved, but the lady didn't wave back. Strange. Maybe it wasn't Izzi, but the long dark hair had certainly looked like her. The lady had stared straight through her, adding to her frustration. Haras felt a pang of rejection.

Izzi hadn't contacted her since she'd left hospital. Haras reminded herself they weren't close friends, so why should she? Maybe they both had an interest in photography, but there was no other reason why Izzi should contact her, except the fact that she'd said she would and she hadn't.

Haras didn't have itchy feet, but she couldn't camp with Renner and Megagem forever. She had grown to love them and would happily have stayed, but she didn't want to overstay her welcome. She also knew there were more paths for her to travel. Where to next, she didn't know, but there was one thing she wanted to do before she left. She wanted to repair the walled garden. That would give her something useful to do, until she came up with another way of finding her father.

On the way to the shower, Haras caught a glimpse of Renner weeding in the garden. What would he think of her gardening plans? Her shower was as fast as her agitated thoughts, and so were her steps into the garden.

"You look as fresh and lovely as my flowers!"

Haras did a little dance. "What a difference a shower makes!" Her new solid white lace blouse was rather beautiful. She ran her finger around the high round neckline feeling the bumpy texture.

"Would you like to do some weeding?" Renner teased.

"Funny," Haras said pulling her long sleeves up below her elbow. 'That's exactly what I want to do."

Renner handed her his gardening fork and Haras laughed. "… but not in this new white blouse. I want to make a xeric garden."

"A what?"

"A garden with drought-resistant plants, ones that don't need to be watered. I want to go back and weed the walled garden near the ancient ruins, *not this garden*." Haras ran her hands through her hair and gazed into the distance.

Renner sat back on his knees.

He pressed his trowel into the soil and gave her his full attention. "So you found it, did you? I can show you the safest path, but if there's no-one to tend the garden, it will end up in the same mess it is now. Are you planning to stay and tend it?"

Haras knew she wasn't, although she didn't say so. She looked at the ground. She wanted to stay just long enough to do that one small thing. It would keep her busy while she waited for an answer from Interpol … and, she might just bump into Nen at the ruins as well. She'd heard he'd been spending time out there, taking photographs and surveying, or some such thing to do with the impact of the earthquake.

"It won't be a small job." Renner said, but Haras was determined to do it.

Renner stood and looked at her silently for a few minutes. "Do you have a list of things you'll need?"

"Not yet. That's my next task."

"Do you need some help with it?"

"No, I should be okay. You could check it when I'm done, and see if I've left anything out."

"I'll take you into town tomorrow, if you like. I need to get some things myself."

Renner was as good as his word. He took Haras into town the following day and she bought a range of tools.

Haras's gardening idea was soon local gossip and it wasn't received well.

At first the negative reaction surprized Haras, and she felt some empathy for the locals. Maybe the thought of what she planned, brought back painful memories of their children, who'd died there. Maybe they didn't want people trampling on the places where their children had spent their last days.

Her empathy was short lived though. It evaporated when the attacks became personal.

"Does she plan to take over the place?"

"Why is she stirring everything up?"

"Who does she think she is?"

"A stranger has no right!"

"*She* doesn't belong here."

As Haras replayed their words, she pressed her lips tightly together and stood with her hands on her hips. She stomped around and fumed. She wasn't going to budge. She was staying put. She had every right to be in Y'kahs. Her grandparents had lived and died here too. That meant she belonged here as much as they did.

More uncharitable thoughts interspersed with doubts, began to create knots in Haras' stomach. The garden belonged to Renner not to them. He'd only given the people the ruins, not the garden. She found herself repeating this in her mind. She could turn it into a xeric garden if she wanted to, if Renner didn't mind, and he didn't mind. They could enjoy it too, if they didn't have such a bad attitude. What did it have to do with them anyway? Old cronies set in their old ways! They weren't camping. They'd built a tomb. She couldn't help laughing at the idea when it popped into her mind, then she felt guilty.

Chapter 11

"Upwards and onwards," Megagem said, but her comment didn't help Haras. She didn't even feel like reading the Bible. Someone had spat on the ground in front of her as she walked past and told her to go back to where she'd come from, again. Why did they hate her? All she wanted to do was make a garden.

Her mind was too full and it was well past midnight when she finally fell asleep. She tossed and turned and didn't sleep long but woke suddenly from a very vivid dream.

In the dream, she was lying on her bed reading a book with her beautiful fluffy white cat beside her. The mattress she was lying on began to rise and carry her over the town. She began to slide off the bed. There wasn't anything to hold on to. She cried out to God in anger.

"Do you want me to die?" She landed safely on her feet on a beach. There were no people around, only a silent sea of water before her. She was still angry.

"What do you want me to do? Do I have to go into the water?" She thought she saw the bones of the dead in it's depths. Her cat had then bounded over to her. She bent to pick her up and realized her cat was lighter than a feather. Her body was already dead, yet she had a life beyond life on earth.

Haras thought about the dream and the walled garden. She was still angry with all the negative responses to what she wanted to do. Then she realized it was what *she* wanted to do. Haras knew she had a choice. She could think the way she'd always thought, travel her worn paths, or she could die to her self-centred thinking and pray like Jesus had. God's will, not hers be done. Some things had eternal value and some didn't.

Haras grumbled to herself that everyone knew she was going to rebuild the walled garden and make it into a xeric one. She'd spent a lot of money on tools and ordered plants. Renner had even organized a friend with a 4WD to take them out there, not Nen. She didn't feel as though she could back down now. What would people think of her if she did? And she hadn't seen Nen since his visit. She'd been hoping he would phone, but he hadn't. She went back to sleep and slept late.

After breakfast, Haras went looking for Renner and Megagem. She found them in the front courtyard by the gate, talking. Their neighbours were saying something about making "Aliyah." They were immigrating to Israel and leaving their old way of life behind. They were even going to leave their old language behind, although not at first, as it would take them a while to speak fluently in Hebrew. They were about to start a brand new life in a completely different country and wanted to say farewell.

When the neighbours were out of earshot, Haras asked Megagem what "aliyah" meant.

"It means to ascend, going up. One never goes down to the Holy City. One always goes up." They played with the up and down theme as they walked back to the house together.

"Down town, up to heaven, down to earth … What about breakfast?" Megagem asked.

"It's already gone down," Haras said.

They laughed.

"Baptism has a lot of the up-down symbolism as well," Megagem said. We go down into the water, letting everyone know we are leaving our old life behind. We come up, symbolising our new life in Christ, our birth into His family. We bury our will and our way of doing things and say yes to what God wants. It's like letting go."

Haras thought of how she felt in her dream as she lost control of the bed. She didn't like the scary feeling.

"Would you like to be baptised, Haras?" Megagem asked.

Haras wanted to say goodbye to her self-centred life. She wanted to do what God wanted, but she felt miserable. She did and she didn't want to let go of what *she* wanted to do.

"I just bought all those tools and told everyone I'm going to clean up the walled garden." Haras pouted. "I know it's what *I* want to do, but what if it isn't what God wants me to do?"

Megagem looked at Haras, and Haras felt as though she was slipping off the mattress and losing control. She waited, hoping Megagem was going to encourage her to make the garden, but she didn't.

"Have you asked God what *He* wants?"

"No."

"God may want you to do it, or He may have something better for you to do. God's plans are always just right. He has dreams for our lives that are always the best. Remember Jesus. He did the will of His Father and that wasn't always easy. There were amazing miracles and great glory, but there was also great pain. Jesus stayed on the right path because he knew it would bring about resurrection life for us. He loved us that much and He still does."

Haras bit her fingernail. It was too hard. She didn't want to ask God in case He didn't want her to do it. What would people think of her if she changed her mind? Some would laugh at her. Some would think she was afraid of them, that they were right, and they had won … and what about Nen? Did God's plans for her include him? She didn't want to let go of the little hold he had on her, in her imaginings. She felt slightly annoyed with Megagem. She lowered her eyes and told her she'd think about baptism and headed back to her room.

Chapter Free

Vexed and irritable, Haras glared at her reflection in the bedroom mirror. "A xeric garden!" She so wanted to make one, and she wanted to see Nen again as well. She'd thought she might see him at church, but he hadn't come.

A xeric garden or a well-watered one?

The comparison suddenly hit her. She could be in a dry place, or one where her thirst was quenched. She was at a crossroad. Would she walk in the ancient path or her own?

Haras let her shoulders sag and took a deep breath. Going her own way was like being her own adversary, building brick walls against the best way. She let go and asked God what He wanted her to do. She would do that!

Joy bubbled up inside, lifting off a wall of heaviness. Why had she been so determined to fix the garden up? Was it because she liked things to be in their place, tidy and orderly? She'd always hated mess. It reminded her of the time her mother had tripped on the mess of boxes she'd made. She knew she liked to be in control, and she wanted to pay Renner and Megagem back, even if they weren't interested in what she wanted to give them. Renner was right. Who would care for the garden if she did fix it up? Even a xeric garden needed some tending … and what about Nen? She talked to God about him too.

During their evening meal, Haras broached the subject. "I don't think I should go ahead with the garden, but what should I do with all the things I bought? You don't need them, do you?" she asked Renner.

"Not really." He was silent for a few moments. "Why not leave them in town with a sign saying 'free.' Secretly giving an angry person a gift is a good proverb and there are a lot of angry people in town."

Haras poked her fried rice. "There sure are - and angry women too!" She could count herself in that category, but wasn't going to say that out loud … but the tools had cost her so much. She didn't want to just give them away, well not to strangers. She wasn't made of money. She looked at Megagem. Her heart softened. She looked at Renner. They'd both given her so much. They might've been rich in land, but they didn't seem to have lots of money, yet they were *so* generous. They were always thanking God for His bountiful provisions.

Haras let go of the cost of the tools. She agreed with Renner. Giving the tools and plants away was a good thing to do.

"I've got some wood and paint for the sign, but first I need to phone the town council. We'll need their permission to put the tools and sign on the park in town."

The following day, with council permission, Renner and Haras went into town early. They didn't want to be seen, but someone was there before them. A black car was parked near the council office, and someone was sitting inside. Haras recognized the dark curly hair. Nen! He was strumming his fingers on the steering wheel, but waved when she looked his way. She waved back then grabbed some tools. He watched for a minute then climbed out.

His clothes were as black as the car. Both looked clean and shining.

"What are you doing? Need a hand Renner?"

Renner put the plants he was carrying down. "Thanks Nen, but no … wouldn't like you to mess your suit. You look like you're heading for an interview."

"No, just work." He walked to the truck, where Haras was attempting to lift a tree. "Hi, Haras. Let me give you a hand with that." She didn't argue. "Are you doing some gardening for the council?"

"No! Don't ask! It's supposed to be a secret ... and please don't tell anyone we left the things here."

"Okay. My lips are sealed!" He zipped them with his fingers. "A mystery?"

Haras changed the subject. "Nice car. Is it new?"

"No, but I've just cleaned it. It's a work car."

Another car pulled into the council drive. Nen looked at his watch. "Right on the dot! I mustn't keep the man waiting." He turned to Haras. "Nice to see you again. I'm staying for the weekend - might see you in church."

"I'll be there."

Nen waved towards Renner and raised his voice. "Good to see you, Renner!" He strode off towards the car.

Haras watched Nen greet the driver. She was still watching as they drove off together. Nen looked back towards her and waved. She waved back.

Renner followed her gaze and Haras felt the colour come into her cheeks.

"Let's get some chocolate cakes and have a special morning tea." Renner said.

"Sounds good to me."

They drove to Klat's store and Haras saw Nellen cleaning the door.

"Hi Nellen. You look busy."

"Hi Haras. Yes. This is the best time of day to do it – not many people about." She finished the door and leaned on the counter. "How are your plans for the walled garden going?"

"I'm not sure I should fix the garden. I'm not going to be around forever and who will look after it when I'm gone?"

The shop assistant stepped back. "What?" She stared at Haras, eyes open wide and said nothing, although her mouth opened and closed a few times. She tightened her lips and threw her cleaning rag into the water bucket. "Don't you let those angry roosters put you off making your xeric garden. It's a lovely idea. Xeric … even the word sounds lovely. I've started one myself."

Haras couldn't help a small grin. She thanked Nellen for her kindness but told her she'd let it go. Renner was right behind her and nodded. He said they had come for some chocolate cakes. Nellen was "fresh out of them," so he put in an order for the following Tuesday.

Thursday, Friday, Saturday …, Sunday at last! Haras changed her mind about what to wear until her room looked a mess of clothes, even though there were only a few of them. Jeans?

Dress? Casual, or classy? She finally chose a black and lime green patterned dress. It suited her necklace and her body perfectly. Modest but stylish.

As she did up her only pair of dressy sandals, she scolded herself. It wasn't a fashion parade. The makeup she hadn't worn for some time came out again. The other girls at church wore it. She would use a little, but only for her lips and eyes. She checked her image in the mirror turning one way then the other. By the time she got to church, she was as nervous as if she was going on a date.

Nen wasn't at church when Haras arrived. She was disappointed. She kept looking out for him, but didn't see him. She had almost given up when he suddenly appeared beside Renner. He leaned round to catch Haras's eye and pointed at his watch. He shook his head as if to scold himself for being so late.

Haras grinned. "Late's okay! The door's still open!"

Haras found it hard to concentrate. She sang without thinking about the words and was very aware of Nen's presence, which distracted her from hearing most of the sermon. She snapped back as the preacher began talking about baptism.

Jesus was baptised. I need to be baptised too.

After the service Nen apologized. "Last to arrive and first to leave." He couldn't stay and chat. His grandfather wanted a ride back to the city and they both needed to stop for groceries on the way. He shook Renner's hand, was hugged by Megagem and looked at Haras. "You look very pretty."

"Thank you," Haras murmured. She'd lost her tongue and she knew she was blushing. Nen tilted his head and started to say something, then stopped. "Must get going." He shook a few hands on the way out and was gone. Assa and Gos were by her side in a flash. They wanted to know all about her relationship with Nen.

"I don't really have one," she said.

"Oh yeah," Gos said. "I heard him say you looked pretty. You're blushing Haras. That's definitely a blush, isn't it Assa"

"Looks like one to me," Assa grinned.

"It's probably my makeup," Haras said.

"I know a blush when I see it," Gos said. "And that's not makeup." They laughed and Haras squirmed.

Chapter 17

"What happened?" Megagem asked Renner when he arrived back from Klat's Store with the chocolate cakes he'd ordered. Both Haras and Megagem looked at each other and then back at him. What was he so amused at?

"Okay," said Megagem "What is it?"

"Wonders never cease!" Renner shook his head again as he put their favourite chocolate cakes on the table. "Amazing … amazing! You will never guess!"

"What *is* it? Spit it out Renner!" Megagem placed her hand on his shoulder.

"Make me a cold drink and I'll tell you," he said, adding to the suspense. He sat down.

Haras got a plate for the cakes and sat down too, eyes glued to Renner's face.

"All the tools are gone," Renner said.

"Well of course," Megagem said.

"You will never guess who took them and what they are going to do with them!" He paused and looked at their faces. "The men at Klat's store asked me what was going on. I told them you were not going to make the xeric garden after all. Nellen then let everyone know how unkind they had been to Haras and how kind she was to give all the tools away. Apparently Nen had been talking to her and some of the men too."

"Nen was talking to Nellen?" Haras's eyes widened and she suspected she was blushing. She quickly lowered her eyes. She didn't want them to see her interest in Nen. Megagem's eyes were glued to her husband's. Haras looked back at him.

"Yes. Nen thought the garden a great idea and you know Nellen had changed her view about it. Well, Nellen told everyone within earshot that you may not have been born in Y'kahs, but your family had lived here and it was time to move on. The blessing of having a loud voice! She said they should have made something beautiful years ago, a memorial for their children, and your xeric garden could be just that. She thought it could be a place of remembrance, a contemplative garden with some seats, so that something good would come from their loss. You should have seen the way the men stared at her. I think I saw all their tonsils!" Renner wiped his eyes. "Then I told them the garden would make a great park. I told them if the town tended it, the town could have it."

Megagem grabbed her mouth to suppress a laugh then shook her head at Renner.

"Nellen soon had them all agreeing. She rounded them up like goats and even her husband backed her up. Nellen and some of those who had complained the loudest are going to help get the garden back in order."

"Oh, that is wonderful," Megagem said.

Haras just sat there, unable to speak. Tears pricked at her eyes but she held them back.

"I knew I should've included the garden with the ruins, given them both to the city." The excitement was gone from Renner's voice. "But I viewed them as mine, as though I was going to be down here forever. I was only thinking of temporary things. Afterwards, I felt guilty and stopped tending it. I thought it was too late."

Everyone was fallible, but Haras couldn't imagine Renner not travelling the ancient paths. She couldn't imagine him holding on tightly instead of giving. She was awed by the wisdom in the Bible. It *was* more blessed to give than to receive. Letting go had started earth quaking changes to Jericho-like walls. A memorial? Yes, the garden would make a great pilgrimage place, a place where people could sit and contemplate.

Haras wiped a tear that had escaped from her eye, and then rubbed them both. On the ancient paths, amazing things happened, not only Godincidents, but also things she'd never dreamed possible.

"Well." Megagem shook her head. "Well." She shook it again.

Haras saw she was lost for words; a rare occurrence. Megagem rubbed her husband's arm and they both wiped their eyes and sat in silence. It was a solemn and awesome moment; another rare occurrence.

Haras felt a deep humility as they continued to sit silently. She was very aware of the presence of God. She broke the silence. She wanted to be baptised and told them both. Renner ran a finger under one eye, then the other. He took out a tissue and blew his nose.

Megagem grinned at Renner. She stood up with arms wide open. "Come here, Haras!"

Just like my mother.

Haras broke the embrace as her phone rang. She left the room to answer it. "Gos! You'll never guess what's just happened!" Gos couldn't, of course, and went into a long discourse on why she couldn't, so Haras had to interrupt her.

"Duh! It's radio Haras here. Are you tuned in?"

"Ha!" Gos stopped to listen and Haras told her the news, about the garden and her decision to get baptised.

"Hey, that's awesome news. Better than mine."

"Yours?"

"Yep I have some news too. I'm not leaving." Haras laughed. "Your feet stopped being itchy?"

"No. Well, a bit. I just phoned to see if you wanted to spend a weekend with me. My parents are going on a cruise and we'll have the place to ourselves. We could plan something awesome."

"Sounds great! Got any ideas?"

"Some," Gos said. "We could have a cook-off, or end–to-end-movies—not really awesome, but anything's possible, right?"

"Right. You, me and God. That's somewhat awesome!" They both laughed and Haras went back into the lounge to finish her coffee. Renner and Megagem were still sitting together. Haras told them about her invitation and they looked at each other and smiled.

Chapter X

Xeric gardening lost the ground it had taken up in Haras's imaginings. She was surprised by just how much time she'd spent in day-dreaming about them and Nen. She began to spend some of the time she'd freed up in talking things over with her heavenly Father again. She had a lot more things to talk to Him about now, including preparing for her baptism. She sent out a few invitations and emailed Izzi one, just in case she was in the country at that time.

Her minister recommended the "Jesus" film and Haras and Gos watched it online towards the end of their awesome-themed weekend.

"Love really is a risky thing, isn't it?" Haras said "Yep," said Gos.

Haras thought it might even be risky telling someone you loved them. Being rejected would hurt. She didn't share this thought with Gos. She didn't want an interrogation on the subject.

"Giving us the freedom to make choices means God suffers the consequences of our selfishness as well as our love," Gos said.

"That's an awesome thought!"

"Did I say that? Wow." Haras and Gos both marvelled and agreed that the weekend had turned out to be an *awesome* one too. They both agreed to plan another weekend, one in the city and another somewhere else, somewhere exciting.

"The ends of the earth … would that be exciting?" Gos asked.

"Too far for a weekend." Haras laughed. "Are you serious? You want to travel?"

"Don't know. Never have travelled. Never really thought about doing so until you came. The idea is kind of growing in me. Tell me about Australia."

"Haven't you heard enough about it?"

"No. Do you think you'll go back and live there?"

"I don't know. Not yet a while anyway. I still need to find my father."

"Will you go live near him?"

"Don't know that, either." Haras thought about Nen and reminded herself that God's paths were her paths. She told Gos she just wanted to follow Christ.

A few days later a letter arrived for Haras. It was postmarked from Lios Doog.

"From the ends of the earth!" Megagem chuckled as she handed it to Haras. "Mail for Renner too," she said and waved it as she left the kitchen.

Haras was all fingers and thumbs. She couldn't open it quickly enough. Was it information from Interpol? She pulled the letter out and looked for the sender.

It was from Natan Revig nee Deerg Anona.

Deerg, her father! It was from her father!

A new name? Why?

She began to read. Interpol had written to him, sent him her letter. He'd recognized her surname and knew the town they said she was living in, otherwise he wouldn't have written.

Oh thank you Jesus.

Haras could hardly read the words. He was married. This didn't sound like the man her mother had spoken about. That Deerg hadn't believed in marriage or God. Was it really her father? She read on.

He'd taken on his wife's name … that explained why he'd been so hard to find.

"You say your mother was Ada? I don't know what she told you, but it was a parting of ideas, ideals and deals to do with the 'I' in each of them"

Haras took a deep breath. *A poet?*

I believed I would find something of great value on the other side of our mountain home. As it turned out there were valleys as deep as the mountain was high, and as deep as the rift between Ada and I. Journeys can be deceptive like that, particularly journeys involving the promise of riches."

Allegories? He sounded a bit like Renner and all his friends when they talked about the ruins. *Promise of riches?* His words sounded like her mother's.

She read on. He regretted breaking up with Ada. Haras regretted it too. When had he regretted it? Why hadn't he gone back to her mother then?

I lost a lot of things I treasured.

What? What had he treasured? Haras felt frustrated. Everything he wrote left her with more questions.

I'm not sure if you are my daughter.

Haras sank into a kitchen chair. Not her father? He must be. She wanted him to be.

She read and reread the letter. She rushed to her room and phoned.

"Ahsha? Sorry to wake you, but I've just received a letter."

Ahsha grunted and Haras told her about the letter.

"Hey, that's great news." Ahsha said.

"It is news, but he doesn't know if he *is* my father."

"What did he say?"

"Well … he said it sounded possible. Oh, and he said he's married. Changed his name too. He took his wife's family name and now he's Natan Revig."

"No wonder no-one's been able to find him."

"He said he didn't know what Mum told me, but it had been a parting of a whole lot of things with *I* in them."

"You mean self?"

"Guess so. He wrote about his break-up with mum like it was a deceptive journey. I wonder if he's a Christian. He says he regretted not going back to Mum. He nearly did, but the prospect of riches pulled him in the opposite direction. He didn't notice the warning signs about the get-rich-quick scheme. He doesn't say what they were. He says he lost a lot of the things."

"That's sad."

"He doesn't elaborate. Wonder if he meant losing his parents … maybe he meant Mum as well, if he is my father that is."

"Sounds like he is. If he didn't think it possible, he wouldn't have written to you."

"Yep, you're probably right. I hope so."

"Send him a photo of the urn."

"Yep, I thought of that too."

"Well I'm so glad for you Haras." She yawned. "I better get back to sleep."

"Sorry, I'm not thinking sensibly. I was so excited and so frustrated. I couldn't wait to tell you."

"That's Okay. That's what good news does, hey?"

"Yep."

"Love you."

"You too. Bye."

Haras wrote back to Natan, telling him about her mother's last words and the section of letter about Elle. She took a photo of the urn and put it in the envelope along with an invitation to her baptism; not that she thought the letter would arrive in time, or that he'd come, but she could hope.

Chapter 11

Yellow icing stuck to Haras's fingers. She licked one savouring the sweet pineapple flavour, before rinsing her hands under the tap and drying them. The cupcakes she'd made looked like sunflowers and Haras was pleased. Hands on hips, she admired them for a while. She was helping Megagem prepare food for her baptismal celebration. It took her mind off her nervousness.

Everyone would be there, watching her - well nearly everyone! Nen wouldn't be there, but he had phoned her. He and a colleague had entered an environmental engineering photography competition. The exhibition opening was the same weekend as her baptism. His parents and grandfather had booked a hotel for the weekend and were looking forward to going. It was going to be a special family celebration, as his parents had been married for thirty years. He was sorry he couldn't make her special day as well.

Finishing the cakes was the final thing on her 'to do' list and she smiled and drew a tick in the air. "Done!" She grinned as she thought of all the preparations. It had been a busy two months. She'd even sent an email invitation to Ahsha, although she'd told her she didn't expect her to come all the way across the world for it. She'd phoned Hannah and she was coming with Reinier, and of course Gos would be there. Gos had promised to try her hand at making Pavlova after Haras had demonstrated how, on their *awesome* weekend.

"This is my baptism, not quite by fire, but by oven," she'd teased Haras. "My pavlova-making baptism; a suitable contribution. It's going to be a work of art. But you must remember it's the thought and the process that counts. Isn't that what you said about art?"

Haras smiled as she remembered and thought about the Pavlova art work Gos was embarking on.

Renner came into the room and stood with his hands on his hips too, staring at all the cupcakes. "My, that makes a pretty picture." He closed his eyes and took a deep breath. "Mmm smells like I'm at Klat's when Nellen's been baking."

"It does, doesn't it?" Megagem said as she put an oven mitt back on its hook. "Haras's done a great job." She wiped her hands on her apron and took it off. "Do you want me to take a photo of you in front of them all?"

"Yes please. I'll get my phone."

Haras rushed out and was soon back, phone in hand.

"Cheeeese. Is that what you say?" Megagem asked and they all laughed.

It was a good photo and soon on its way to Ahsha with the text, "This is what you'll be missing."

The following day Haras woke early but was so excited and nervous she couldn't eat breakfast.

They carried all the prepared food to the car and took it to the church hall. The room had been set up the day before and Haras was pleasantly shocked at the fresh whiteness of the tablecloths. The smell of lavender sprigs among the flowers on each table, took her back across the world, to a flower shop she'd loved to browse in. They dusted any hint of stale air right out the open windows.

"Beautiful, isn't it," Megagem whispered near her ear.

"Embracing," Haras said and stood still a moment longer to drink it all in.

The church was fuller than normal when they walked in, and as Haras moved towards the front, she saw someone with long blonde hair. She stared hard at the lady's back, puzzling as to who it could be. Blonde hair was a rarity in Y'kahs. It looked like Ahsha. The lady turned around.

Haras couldn't believe it. It was Ahsha! She ran to her and they both hugged and laughed and wiped the moisture from their eyes.

Haras wanted to ask her lots of questions. How had she drummed up the courage to fly so far? It wasn't like her at all. Fearful Ahsha? There was no time. Lots of people wanted to shake her hand and welcome her and she still had to go out the back and change into a white robe.

Gos caught her eye and held up her thumb. She nodded and mouthed the word Pavlova. Haras was glad it had turned out and gave her the thumbs up back, before being whisked away to change.

As the service began, Haras noticed the art work at the front had been changed. It was new. It looked like her favourite song, a tambourine with ribbons flowing like water down a mountain. The river spray was filled with clapping hands.

Haras looked around and thought she felt as full of family as anyone ever could, even without her earthly father.

The minister was calling her. She was shaking as she approached the baptismal font; a round inflatable pool hired for the occasion. Haras shared her testimony and climbed into the water.

"Haras, in baptism today, you are going public, and viral, by the looks of those phones."

Everyone laughed. The minister chuckled. "As you go down into the water, you will be drowning your present name and your old life. You will come up out of the water, and life will no longer be about what you can do, but what Christ can do in and through you."

Haras felt her heart leap. The dream! No wonder she'd been angry in the dream, asking what she had to do. Her focus was misplaced. It wasn't about her. It was all about Jesus.

"I will baptise you in water, and Jesus will baptise you with the Holy Spirit. You will come out of the water with a new name, a Christian name. Sarah, which means princess," the minister said. "This will be a permanent reminder that you are a new creature in Christ, a member of God's royal household.

"Sarah?" Haras heard the surprise as some realised what she was doing. She had organised her name change before-hand, but had kept it a secret.

"I baptise you Sarah Anona, in the name of the Father, the Son and the Holy Spirit."

Sarah came up out of the water and everyone began singing her favourite river song. Her heart sang it too, like a river overflowing.

Chapter 

Zipping up her dress was more difficult with cold fingers. Sarah was glad Ahsha was there to help. She did the necklace up too, talking non-stop. They had so much to catch up on. Texting and FaceTime wasn't the same.

Sarah's stomach growled. She was hungry. A quick fluff of the towel through her hair, a comb and lipstick, and she was ready for food. Together they walked to the church hall.

Everyone wanted to be introduced to Ahsha and to talk to Sarah about her name change. Ahsha was soon surrounded by a group of male admirers, so Haras headed for the food. She would take Ahsha one of her cupcakes and rescue her, hungry or not.

"Hello Sarah."

She stopped in her tracks. It was Izzi.

"Izzi! I didn't see you. When did you get here?"

"I was a little late. Slipped in just before you slipped under the water. Just made it." Her long black hair hung loosely, covering her back like a veil, which gave it the appearance of being part of her sleek fitting boot-cut, leather outfit.

"I'm so glad you could make it."

Gos approached and handed Haras a plate of Pavlova.

"I saved you some, princess."

"Wow. That's some baptismal outcome!" Sarah laughed.

"Yeah. It turned out well." She looked at Izzi. "Introduce me!"

"Gos, this is Izzi, Izzi, Gos." Haras didn't elaborate on her real name. It had slipped from her mind. "I met Izzi on the plane coming here and she visited me in hospital. She drops into Y'kahs from time to time when she's not in Paris or some other exotic place around the world."

Izzi laughed. "Less glamourous than you make it sound."

Gos pouted. "Sounds pretty good to me. I've never been out of Y'kahs."

"Why not?" Izzi asked.

"Well … why not! Never thought of it like that. I will have to do something about it now."

Sarah took a spoon full of Pavlova. "Mmm, better than my mother's."

"Rubbish. You said your mother's always turned out perfectly. I need a bit more practice, I think. Looks great though doesn't it? A real work of art … cream and chocolate - couldn't find strawberries."

"It's awesome." They both laughed.

"Hey Gos, what's the news?" It was Hannah. She linked arms with Gos, who introduced her to Izzi. They immediately hit it off.

Gos was full of news and as Sarah listened, she noticed a well-dressed man with dark hair and smooth olive skin, staring at her. She couldn't take her eyes from his glowing face as he approached with Renner.

"Natan, this is Haras, I mean Sarah," Renner said. "I can see the family likeness."

Natan held out his hand and Sarah took it, forgetting to shake it. His soft brown eyes wrinkled at the corners and her heart began to pound. She didn't know what to say. He spoke first.

"I recognized the urn," he was saying. "But it was the photo of you on the invitation that convinced me. I couldn't believe how much you look like my mother. You are a surprise!"

"I didn't think you'd come." Sarah was surprised how tiny and quiet her words came out. She cleared her throat. "I wasn't sure the letter would even get to you in time." Her eyes were watering.

"Just in time," he said. "Perfect timing. Another day and there wouldn't have been enough time for all the travel arrangements."

Sarah knew what that was like. "Everyone says I look just like Elle, your mother."

"Yes, I think you do. I see you're wearing her necklace. My mother gave it to me when I told her about the vows I'd made to your mother. Did you know it belonged to her?"

Sarah nodded. "Tell me about it." She put the rest of her sandwich in her mouth.

"My mother, Elle found the necklace in her doll when I accidentally broke it. She showed Grandma, and the long and short of it is, Grandma told Elle she'd been adopted. Australia was thought to be a safe place at the beginning of the war and a lot of children, many orphaned from Europe, had been shipped over. Apparently, Elle was too young to remember she'd been adopted. She came with a small suitcase and a doll. He paused and reached for a sandwich. "These look good!"

"Yes, Megagem made them. She's a great sandwich maker and cook." Haras wiped her eyes. "Weren't you interested in finding her birth mother?"

"At the time, I was preoccupied with your mother, not mine." Natan took a bite. "The stone in the middle of the necklace is different. It had a heart in it when I gave it to your mother, as I remember."

Sarah told him about the stone she'd found in the urn and how she'd replaced the heart. She turned the stone over.

Natan turned his gaze to Sarah's face. "We all have new hearts to match the necklace."

"Yes, ancient ones." Sarah paused for a moment as she realised what he'd said. Did he recognize the ancient source of their new life and change of heart too? "So you are a Christian?"

"I am."

Sarah ran her finger over the silver band. "Is that why you changed your name and took on your wife's surname?"

"Yes. My first name really did capture the kind of person I used to be. When I became a Christian, like you, I wanted to say goodbye to that person. Natan means God has given."

Natan finished his coffee and placed the cup on the table. He twisted the gold band on his ring finger. "When I was first introduced, I was rather taken with my wife's name. Right from that first meeting it seemed she was meant for me and I for her."

"Wow. Caught by a name." Gos laughed as Hannah walked away to join Ahsha.

"Some names are powerful." Sarah bumped against Gos.

Gos laughed again. "Yeah. Jesus for sure. Must let you two catch up." She took another sandwich and left.

Natan took another sandwich as well. "So, Sarah, you wrote about a letter saying something about my mother having a sister?"

"Yep. If so, she might still be alive and still wondering what happened to Elle."

"Mmm." Natan nodded as he swallowed his mouthful. "My mother did think she had a sister somewhere—."

Megagem joined them. "Hello. Did I hear you say a sister?"

Sarah put her arm around Megagem. "Megagem's my second mother."

Natan wiped his hands on a paper napkin and held out his hand. "Natan Revig."

"I'm so glad to meet you," Megagem said. She held on to his hand and patted it with her free one.

"Sarah just told me her mother said something about a sister."

"A possible great aunt." Megagem said. "More family?" She beamed at both of them.

"More seeking!" Sarah laughed.

"And more finding, perhaps?"

"What's this about more seeking?" Renner said as he re-joined them.

"My mother was adopted." Natan said. "She told me she thought she had a sister. She remembered the two of them singing together. She was on a pilgrimage to find her."

"Sounds like Haras here," Renner said.

"Not the singing bit," Haras laughed.

"He means you both came to Y'kahs," Megagem said.

"Why did she come to Y'khas?" Sarah asked.

Natan took a deep breath. "I told her I was stuck here for some time. I was waiting to be a witness in a court case," He looked at Renner and Renner nodded slowly.

"I heard about that." Haras said. "Ramar Krad's grandson, Nen told me."

Renner stared blankly at Haras.

"He ..." Haras pressed her lips together. It wasn't the right time to talk about Ramar Krad.

"My mother told me she'd travel to the ends of the earth to find her sister, and so she did travel, I mean across the world. She didn't live long enough to find her sister, though."

"That's sad," Megagem said.

Natan nodded and his faced looked as sad as hers. "I was too self-centred in those days and not interested in searching. Then I got married and busy with work and children -two boys." He smiled.

"Two boys." Megagem patted Haras's arms. "You have two step brothers."

Haras didn't know what to say. What would that be like? Would they like her? Would she like them?

"My wife has enough extended family to keep us busy. I regret neglecting the search."

"It may not be too late, and finding people is a lot easier these days," Megagem said.

"Yes … but first, I have so much to find out about Sarah! I missed so much of her life." He turned to Sarah. "I'm glad I was able to get here in time for your baptism. It's special to you. That makes it special for me, too."

Sarah caught a glimpse of her heavenly Father's love in his eyes. His kindness reached right down into her heart, melting the remnants of anxiety and loneliness that suddenly seemed to have been forever around her heart. For a moment she felt like a princess; someone of great value because she knew she'd found great treasure, not only her heavenly Father, but also her earthly father. And they both treasured her.

Hi there,

Although this story is fiction and none of the characters are real, some of the events like the healing really did happened to someone, just as they are described. Sometimes the truth is harder to believe than fiction. Were there some things you thought were purely fictional?

Alphabetical acrostics can be found in the Hebrew Bible. Did you work out the message I hid in the middle of the acrostics? Seekers Finders.

Many other literary features are used. Can you find examples of alliteration and similes? Are they helpful? Did any of the proper nouns help you understand the characters better? If not, then read them from right to left. Some are palindromes.

There are a few themes in this story including treasure. Do treasure and trash ever have anything in common? What could have made Haras believe her father treasured her? What do you treasure? What do you think is the greatest treasure?

If you enjoyed this story and want to continue with Haras on her journey of seeking and finding, you will enjoy the next book in this series –Follow the ancient path

Jennifer Phillips

Meaning of Names

Anona - pineapple possible derived from Roman Goddess believed to be a guardian of harvest and food supplies.
Ahsha – desire or life
Hannah – she knows
Natan – he gave
Nen – ancient waters
Renner – messenger, runner
Nellen – horn
Maham – full moon
Eve – live, woman
Bob – bright, glory
Nayan – cave
Nosson – bitter, beloved
Masam – sour

Haras - Sarah
Releah – Healer
Revig – Giver
Y'kahs – Shaky

If you enjoyed *Find The Ancient Path* and want to find out more, there are two more books in draft form. The working titles are: *The Hiding Song* and *Follow The Ancient Path*

In order to escape their war torn homeland two girls are given new names and begin a dangerous journey to the land of freedom. Will they both arrive safely? What will they find there?

Author

Jennifer Kathleen Phillips
GradDipTh, BEd, DipIT, DipTchg, TTC

Jennifer Phillips is a Christian author and has been a member of a number of organisations including the Gold Coast Writers Association and the Australian Federation of Graduate Women. She is a registered teacher and has developed courses, including a successful early reading program. She has taught all ages and authored a number of books covering a range of subjects. She is internationally known for her unique forms of poetry. She was awarded the university title of Massey Scholar, and has won awards in other fields as well as academic writing.